I MOBSTER

I MOBSTER

JOSEPH HILTON SMYTH
(WRITING AS "ANONYMOUS")

CUTTING EDGE

ISBN-13: 978-1-970848-00-7

Published by
Cutting Edge Books
PO Box 8212
Calabasas, CA 91372
www.cuttingedgebooks.com

CHAPTER ONE

W HO CAN remember when it started?

Maybe it was when I was six or seven. It must have been summer. It was a hot day, anyway, because the street was crowded, folks sitting on the stoops and in the open windows and kids swarming over the sidewalks. On the top step across the street a fat woman was nursing a baby and yelling up at a neighbor in a third-floor window. In the areaway beside the steps a couple of old greasers were playing dominoes, shouting and swearing at each other. I was sitting on the edge of the curb, not doing anything except in my mind. Whatever it is a kid six, seven thinks about. All around is the stink of the gutters and rotting garbage and the heavy, sweaty smell of too many people. A smell I never did get out of my nostrils, that not even a hundred-dollars-a-day sea breeze at Miami could ever sweep completely away.

That was when the sounds came that were different somehow from the other sounds of the street. I didn't know then what gunshots sounded like, but I had a funny feeling inside of me that this new sound was important.

I turned my head just as the man who ran the olive-oil store next door came running out. He had his hands tight to his belly and he couldn't run straight, kind of staggering from side to side until finally he tripped over himself and fell.

That was when I saw the two men behind him. Both of them had guns, but they weren't running. Just moving slowly, as if they knew there wasn't any hurry. They leaned over the man on the sidewalk and he started to cry up at them in Italian and then his words choked off. One of the men laughed and pointed down with the gun in his hand. I heard the sounds again and on the sidewalk the man's head made funny, jerky movements. Then he didn't have a face any more—just blood-red meat like in the butcher store.

And I heard the quiet.

I never heard so much quiet so quick. All the shouting and yelling, all the sounds and noises that were always part of the street were gone. The sidewalks and steps were empty, like folks had never been there at all. There wasn't any more stick-ball game in the middle of the street. Nothing moved except halfway down the block where there was a brewery wagon waiting in front of the bar. The big horses were tired of standing, or maybe didn't like what was happening. They started slapping their front hoofs down on the pavement and it sounded almost like the guns had sounded.

I got up and began moving toward the olive-oil man. Somebody screamed at me, but it wasn't in the Sicilian my old lady used, so I didn't pay it no mind. I got over alongside the body and looked down, trying to figure out what had happened. There was still blood moving and dripping a little, but that was all. No other movement.

Then I heard something that I recognized—the shrill screech of a police whistle and the sound of a night stick beating against the wall of a building. I looked up and saw the blue uniform pounding down from the corner of the avenue. The same moment someone grabbed me from behind and lifted me off my feet and hauled me into the pizzeria next door to the olive-oil store. A couple of men started yelling at me don't I know enough to get off the street when I should and slapping me across the face. Then the old lady that runs the joint started screaming they should quit, and then came over and shoved a big slice of pizza in my hands.

It was about two minutes later that the cops came storming in wanting to know where the kid was that saw the shooting.

All they got for an answer was a lot of shrugs.

Then one spotted me and came over and stuck a finger in my face and began shouting. What did I see? Was I there when it happened? What did the men look like? How many were there?

I had a mouth full of cheese and tomato. I couldn't talk. I could just stand wide-eyed against the wall while the old lady screamed back at the cops.

"You crazy mens? What you bother with little kid for? He don't see nothing!"

So after some more yelling back and forth, with the old lady shouting the loudest, the cops gave up. When they were gone the old lady gave me a whack on the head.

"You hear what I say, Tony? You don't see nothing. You don't say nothing. That way you never get in no troubles."

I swallowed the rest of the pizza and ducked another slap. There was still a lot of excitement out on the sidewalk, with cops swarming like flies all over the place, so I stayed in the store.

I stayed close to the counter, and when nobody was looking I grabbed another piece of pizza. I had it half eaten before the old lady caught me, and even then she was too busy peering through the glass of the front door to do more than call me names.

After that for a long time I sat on the same curb in the same place every day, waiting for the same thing to happen again.

Every time I felt hungry I started wishing somebody would start shooting guns. I kept thinking of those big pieces of pizza I got for nothing.

So what do you remember?

I didn't have the words for it then, but later I read them somewhere. It was like being born in the jungles—the city jungles of dirt and filth and stinking rat traps they called houses. You had to be on the lookout all the time, just to be let alone. Sticking your head outdoors first, giving the street a quick once-over like an alley cat on the prowl. Making sure everything was safe.

That's the way it was if you were a runt like me, with nobody bigger to go to bat for you if you got pushed around. There was just me and the old lady. The old man didn't count. He had a job in a macaroni factory and after supper every night he went down to the back room of a wop grocery store around the corner and sat and played cards and drank wine with some other old *paisanos*. He didn't know but about three English words, and he didn't want to know more than that. He might just as well have stayed in Sicily.

So I learned what the score was, soon as I was old enough to be out on the streets. You had to know or you didn't last long. Everything was a fight—a fight just to exist. A fight just to mind your own business. Stand with a couple of other kids on the street corner, doing nothing or maybe pitching pennies or building a bonfire. Comes a flatfoot snarling, "Break it up! Get out of here before I crack your heads in."

Or comes the gang from the next block, looking to give you a beating just for the hell of it.

The answer was to belong. You had to get accepted by the kid mob that ran the block or you were on your own. You were on the outside without protection.

Me, I was a runt. Always undersized for my age, even after I grew up. I wasn't any good in gang fights, so I had to look for other angles. But I could run and I got to be expert at lifting stuff—little things like cigarettes and candy out of the stores and fruit off the pushcarts. So I was taken in because I could pay my way.

That's how Big Sam happened to latch onto me as a side-kick. He was a couple of years older than me and about twice my size. Big, but slow in the head. I was sitting on the steps one day, not doing anything, when he came down the sidewalk and stopped. We passed a few words and then he asked, "You got a smoke, kid?"

I shook my head. He started to move away and I got an idea. I guess I didn't want to be left alone again. Or maybe I just wanted to show off.

"Wait here and I'll get some."

I took off for the grocery around the corner. I waited until some woman started in with a shopping bag and eased in after her. There was only one clerk, and as soon as he got busy filling the woman's order I went to work. The cigarettes were on a shelf at the end of the counter, within easy reach when the guy's back was turned. There were some boxes of sweet cookies on a table by the door and I sneaked a couple of them inside my shirt for good measure. Then I high-tailed it out.

Big Sam was still waiting. I tossed him a package of cigarettes and he opened it and took one and started to hand it back. I shook my head.

"Keep them. I got some for myself, too." I drew a box of cookies out of my shirt. "While I was about it I got us something to eat."

He gave a pleased whistle.

"You did all right, kid. Me, I ain't no good snitching stuff. I always get spotted."

I shrugged. "It's easy. You gotta know how, that's all. Maybe it helps some being small like I am."

He nodded, stuffing himself with the cookies like he hadn't eaten for a week. I took out the other box and handed it to him.

"Stick this in your shirt for later."

"You're all right, Tony."

The way he said it made me feel good. Important. Not just on the fringe any more.

"Any time," I said. "Any time you want something you let me know, Sam."

So from then on I had a friend. The way it was when we were kids was the way it stayed later, all through the years. I did the thinking and the planning and the tricky stuff. Big Sam was the muscle. The strong arm. The enforcer.

That was back in the days when street fights were a dime a dozen. The East Side was just one great big battle-ground. There was the Five Points Gang and Monk Eastman's outfit and Dopey Benny Fein's mob. Where we lived was in the middle of everything. It was a wop neighborhood, but the Jews crowded in on one side and the micks on the other. There didn't have to be grown-up excuses for fights—it was enough just that there was a difference. The wops and micks both ganged up on the Jew boys, and when that was over the wops and micks would have it out because they were different kinds of Catholics. And inside our own neighborhood we fought in between times. The Sicilians looked down on the Neapolitans, and both of them took it out on the dumb Calabrians. Even when it didn't lead to fighting, your ears got tired of listening to all the dialects you got screamed at you.

So I grew up with the street for a school. The street and in the stinking hot nights of summer the roofs and the rickety fire escapes. There aren't any secrets in the slums. You only had to look to see kids being born and old folks kicking off. Sit in the dark on a fire escape and watch through a window while grown-ups undressed and got into bed.

Even when he was only about twelve or thirteen Big Sam used to get excited, just watching, and right away he'd want to go and do likewise.

"Go on up on the roof," he'd whisper. "I'll be back in a couple of minutes."

I'd go up on the roof and wait in the dark shadows of the chimney. It would be maybe ten, fifteen minutes, and then he'd appear with Angie or one of the other neighborhood girls. I think it was Angie the first time. She wasn't more than my age—about eleven. She was nervous and frightened and not liking being there at all.

"What you drag me up here for, Sam? You let me go or I'll tell—"

He slapped her. "You ain't telling nobody. You want I should spread it about how I caught you yesterday with your dress up rubbing bellies with Louie Ricca?"

"That was diffrunt."

"Do it to one, do it to all," Sam said flatly. He pushed her back down on the rough tarpaper roof.

She was wearing black cotton stockings that made the rest of her legs look milky white in the darkness once he got her drawers off. She kept squirming and half pleading, "I ain't never done it."

"Tell that to Louie next time," Sam grunted.

I guess nothing actually happened. We just went through the motions. I remember feeling kind of let down and disappointed, wondering why older guys were always bragging and boasting of having done it to this one and that. But I couldn't say so out loud. I had to act grown-up and agree along with Sam that it was hot stuff.

Maybe Sam really thought so. That was all he ever thought about. Food and girls. Filling his gut first and then going with some dame. Even later, when there was plenty of money rolling in for anything and everything, that was all he cared about. No imagination. In a way that was all right, too, for it made him tops as a killer. He didn't get nervous from thinking about the job too much ahead of time or panicky remembering afterward. He just went ahead and did it and forgot about it.

No imagination, but dependable. A real nice guy and a good friend. The only honest one I ever had.

Back in those days it was Cherry Nose Petrucci who headed up the kid mob in the neighborhood. He was older than the rest of us, maybe fifteen, and not too bright. But his big brother was important—he owned the wine store in the block and had some kind of connection with the wholesale produce market downtown. According to whispers, he was on the inside of the Maffia, too, although that was something it wasn't healthy to talk about out loud.

It was because of his brother that Cherry Nose had power and knew certain things. Things like how to handle the cops. Some you could talk back to, if you were in Cherry Nose's mob, and others you had to duck, no matter who you were with. All of them were bad news, any way you looked at it. Cheap, chiseling grafters, living fat off the neighborhood like leeches—always taking, taking, and then coming back and asking for more.

Sometimes there would be an honest one, and he'd be the worst of all. Mean and nasty and ugly because he hadn't got anyplace in twenty, thirty years, because he was too stupid to know how to take it in and pay it out in the right places. Like the big red-faced mick we used to call Scratch-Ass Kelly, on account of how he used to stand flat-footed at the call box on the corner, scratching his behind and glaring in four directions at the same time, looking for somebody to lay into with his night stick. Looking for a way to work off his meanness.

Or maybe it would be a young punk, thinking he was a tin god because he had himself a badge and a uniform.

I grew up hating the cops. Watching them as a kid shaking down the little grocery stores that stayed open on a Sunday to make an extra buck, watching them put the bite on the bar where maybe there was a little card game going on in the back room, watching them put the squeeze on the poor broken-down whores that hung out on the corner of the avenue at night looking to make four bits for a flop. Always they were looking for something out of line, so they could get their cut.

Cops and politicians. All my life, even before I was out of knee pants, I've been paying them off. Most of the things I've done, most of the rackets I've worked, wouldn't have been possible without a fix—a pay-off all up and down the line.

So I've paid, and paid plenty. From the first two bucks I had to pay off to the corner flatfoot when I started working the pushcarts to the twenty grand I had to lay on the line last year for a stiff-necked old politician down in Washington to buy a pardon for one of my boys on an old narcotics rap, to keep him from being deported.

You keep paying out, but you can't trust them from one day to the next. When the chips are down, the cops and politicians are all alike. They'll rat and turn yellow and do anything to save their stinking hides.

Like the way they treated Lepke.

But all that came later. In the beginning all I knew was the street and the neighborhood and how far it was safe to go alone without getting caught by some Jew or mick gang. Sometimes, if one of our mob had been beaten up, Cherry Nose got us all together and we went off on a gang fight, armed with bricks and bottles and knives. Sometimes he would have more important things for us to do, like when election time would roll around. Then we'd get paid for busting up rallies—things like heaving rotten vegetables at the opposition speakers on some corner soapbox or tossing stink bombs in the trucks that carted the wrong candidates around.

Come election day, just before the polling booths closed at night we'd be rounded up by Cherry Nose and sent to bust in the place, shouting and yelling and raising hell. Then in the excitement while we were being chased out the right parties could go ahead stuffing the ballot boxes.

But mostly we were on our own. There wasn't a lot of loose money lying around, as there is today, and we had to scratch for nickels and dimes. We learned the usual things kids learn. There were always drunks stretched out on the street late at night, particularly over toward the Bowery, and if we were lucky we got to them before someone else had rolled them. Mostly they didn't have much money left by then, but now and then we'd get a break and roll a lush who had a watch or a good pair of shoes—something we could peddle to the secondhand store around on First Avenue.

There was a whore house on the next block and Sam got to hanging around outside, watching the men go in and out. Watching and wishing he was older. It seemed like a waste of time to me, and then one day I got an idea.

After that we'd wait on the sidewalk until some customer came slinking out and then we'd brace him.

"How about a quarter, mister? Give us a quarter, huh?"

One out of five would maybe come across without any argument. The rest would snarl and keep on going.

We'd follow them down the street, chanting, "He's been to Mamie's cat house. He's been to Mamie's cat house. He got a lay and had to pay at Dirty Mamie's cat house...."

Usually he'd come across then, red-faced and angry and calling us dirty names as he flung the change at us.

But it was bad for Mamie's business. Word got back to her what we were doing and she lay in wait for us. We were out on the sidewalk late one afternoon, looking for a customer to come out, when the front door opened and Mamie herself stuck her head out and beckoned.

"You kids want to make a dollar running an errand?"

"What kind of an errand?"

"Come up here and I'll tell you. I ain't yelling my business all over the street."

So we eased up the front steps. She'd stepped back into the hallway, leaving the door open, and we went in. I looked around quickly, maybe expecting to see a lot of naked dames like in the postcards Louie the Gimp was always showing around. But it was just like the inside of any other house.

Then the front door slammed shut and Mamie grabbed us both by the shirt front.

"What you two little snot-nosed brats think you're doing? Trying to ruin my business?"

Sam didn't say anything. He was just staring bug-eyed at Mamie. She was a big woman, with yellow hair and a lot of red on her cheeks and lips. She was wearing some kind of kimono, and when she gave us a shake it came half open and you could see about everything.

I said, "The street's free, ain't it? We're not asking you for nothing."

She gave us another shake. "I'll give you something without you asking for it. I ought to beat the ass off both of you."

Sam kind of smiled at her. "You want I should take my pants down now?"

Mamie stared at him hard. Then she had to laugh. "I'm not running a kindergarten yet, sonny. And I won't be running anything if you two little bastards don't leave my trade alone. First it's the cops I've got to pay off, then the pimps, and now it's kids in knee pants yet. An honest woman can't make a decent living no more."

In the end we made a dicker. We wouldn't bother her customers any more, but after school every day we'd come around and run errands for her and her girls. Whatever errands there were—like getting magazines and cigarettes and stuff from the drugstores. Mamie would give us half a buck a day each.

"I don't get it," Sam complained after we'd left. "We was making that much without doing any work at all. How come you wanted it this way? It don't add up."

Sure it added up, I told him. Most of the things Mamie had mentioned, like cigarettes and magazines and fancy powders, we wouldn't have to pay for. We could snitch them easy, like we'd been doing all along, and keep the money for ourselves. It would amount to a lot more than any buck a day between the two of us.

Big Sam slapped me hard on the shoulder. "Jeez, Tony, you think of everything. You got a smart head."

"You got to think of the angles," I said, feeling pleased but trying not to show it. "All the time you got to think of the angles."

"You and me together, Tony. We'll do all right."

One way or another we got by. With Big Sam at my side and change in my pocket, I felt safe and secure. It didn't matter any more about being a runt, spindly and undersized. I'd found a way of equalizing things. Other kids started hanging around because if I felt like it I could blow them to sweet pop at the candy store or buy a string of tickets to the nickelodeon over on Second Avenue.

It's a funny thing about money, and the feeling of power money brings when you start spreading it around. After a while there is never enough—you keep wanting and needing more. Not for yourself, not just to spend selfish, but to keep people looking up to you. To keep them asking. Without money you are nothing—just a bum having to belong to some other guy's mob to get by. Taking orders and picking up the leavings. On your own you don't carry any weight.

Big Sam would have been contented with the money we were making off Mamie's joint and from rolling drunks and stuff like that. But for me it wasn't enough. It was just change, and I wanted folding money. The kind that's important.

So I'm about twelve when I get a brain wave. It wasn't mine, I stole it from listening to a couple of older guys that worked for a protective outfit. At the time they were bringing pressure on the pizzeria joints. These two guys smashed windows. The idea was a pizzeria either joined the protective association or things happened. Smashed windows to begin with, and then stink bombs, and if that didn't work then a different kind of bomb.

All of a sudden I think of the pushcarts lined up around on the avenue. We kids had been stealing from them since who knows when. Swooping down in a gang and grabbing up stuff and scattering. Complaining to the cops didn't do the peddlers any good. Even if there was a flatfoot around, he couldn't chase a dozen kids going off in as many different directions.

Now I had an idea. I took Big Sam and we went around to where the pushcarts were lined up and I put the proposition straight. Did they want to stop losing stuff? Did they want to stop having to fight off kid raids all the time?

One buck a week it would cost.

The first day we don't line up so many. About eight or ten, all told, the kind of easy touches who will say yes to anything if it looks like a way to stay out of trouble. But that was enough to start with.

Then I go and hunt up Cherry Nose, who still gives orders to the gang.

"Pretty soon we don't bother the pushcarts no more," I said. "We pass the word around to lay off."

He looked at me impatiently. "You got rocks in the head?"

"For ten bucks a week I got rocks. That's what I kick back to you."

He gave me another look. A sawbuck in those days, back toward the beginning of the first war, was money. Even to a sixteen-year-old guy like Cherry Nose it was important dough. So he stopped making cracks and. listened. Then I took him around on the avenue and pointed out the peddlers who had signed up.

After that things started happening to the others—the ones who had given me the brush-off. Kids got into phony gang fights near them and they got tipped over by accident. Garbage and junk landed on them from the roofs alongside. One thing after another.

They got the point. By the end of the week I had about thirty pushcarts on my list. I'm collecting thirty bucks a week and paying out ten of that to Cherry Nose.

Then some holdout squawks to the law, and one Friday when I'm collecting, the flatfoot on the beat grabs me. So there's a song and dance about what do I think I'm doing and how he ought to run me in and give me a taste of the reform school or anyway bat my ears off. And I stick to my story I'm collecting for running errands and who can prove different?

The windup is I go around the corner with him and give him a couple of bucks.

Twelve years old and already I'm paying off the cops.

But they let me keep the racket going.

Things were better then for a while. I had other kids follow-ing me around, waiting after school, wanting to do this and that. I didn't have to chase after anybody any more—they came to me. Was we playing stick ball or something in the street, I'd be cap-tain of one side automatic.

But I learned better than to stick my neck out that way. It never pays to head up a side that might lose, even in a game.

"Let Luigi be captain," I'd say. Or Rocco or Steve or Frank, It didn't matter. I'd sit on the steps and watch. Then if our side lost they'd figure they let me down.

It was smarter that way than playing myself.

Other guys wanted to pal around with me, but I stuck to Big Sam. We were a team, like, always together. Even when we didn't have anything to do we'd go off by ourselves, as if we had some-thing private cooking.

On the warm summer nights we'd go up on the roof and smoke and look up at the stars, planning out loud what we were going to do when we grew up.

"I'm going to buy me a restaurant in town. And upstairs I'm going to have rooms filled with dames. Not no broken-down whores like at Mamie's, but real classy ones. Broadway show girls, maybe. All blondes. All for me. What you want, Tony?"

"A million dollars."

"Yeah. But when you get it, then what?"

I tried to think. I thought of Moran, the lousy flatfoot who was always waiting for me on Friday to shake me down. He wasn't contented with two bucks a week any more. He'd wanted three, and now he was asking for four. Telling me he was getting too many complaints. Acting like I was working for him, maybe, instead of myself.

"I'll buy guns and give them away all over the town," I said. "I'll spread the word around that I'll pay a thousand bucks for every goddamned cop anybody kills."

Big Sam said, "Jeez, a thousand bucks!"

"That's right. On the line."

"Give me a thousand bucks and I'll go kill one for you, Tony. For a thousand bucks right now I'll kill you a dozen."

Daydreams. Just the stuff kids think about growing up. Plans that usually don't ever get beyond words—just something to take the emptiness out of the future.

But the way it happened, Big Sam got his restaurant. His restaurant and his blonde show girls and all the other things that had looked so important back then.

I got my million dollars.

A lot of cops got killed, too. Not enough, though. Let a cop get killed, and no matter what kind of a lousy bastard he is there's too much of a stink.

CHAPTER TWO

'M STILL going to school, but the stuff I learn there don't amount to much. Reading I didn't mind, and figures always came easy to me. Without being able to count and figure percentages you'd get taken over in no time in one of the alley crap games, and if you didn't have a memory you might just as well forget about playing rummy. It didn't look so good being bad at those things.

But for the rest, school didn't count. It was just something you had to do or put up with a lot of grief from cops and truant officers coming around to the house and asking questions. So it was a place to sit six, seven hours a day. In our school there was kind of an armed truce. We didn't bother the teachers none and they didn't bother us. Come the end of the year we were passed anyway, whether we'd learned anything or not.

Glad to get rid of us, I guess.

Once in a while a new teacher came in with fancy ideas about changing things and being strict. That never lasted long. Was it a man teacher, we'd get some of the older boys in the neighborhood to gang up on him on his way home, pushing him around and picking a fight. Was it a woman, there was different ways. We'd pass the word along so that the guys on the street corners would call names after her and make suggestions, with gestures how she could make a half a buck quick. Usually a woman teacher with ideas about being strict got herself transferred quick out of the neighborhood.

So the way it worked, school wasn't any trouble.

It was outside that you learned most of the things that mattered. Learned them the hard way, so that the lessons stayed taught. I didn't figure it that way in the beginning—they were just rules you had to go by in order to keep your nose clean.

Like the time Cherry Nose came to me to come up with twenty bucks quick.

"You heard about Rocco Calicci?"

"I seen it in the papers."

That had been about a week before. This Calicci and a couple of other guys had busted into a cigarette warehouse. The watchman was supposed to be an old bastard who would be easy to handle, but it hadn't worked out that way. He had put up a fight and someone had blasted him down. Maybe it was Calicci who killed him. Anyway, he was the only one of the three who got caught.

"He needs dough," Cherry Nose said. "It's going to cost plenty to get the rap cut down."

"I don't know him. He ain't even from this neighborhood."

"That don't make no difference. He's a wop, ain't he? They passed the word down from the top that everybody should kick in. That's what my brother told me."

I still wasn't sold. It was winter, and there weren't many pushcarts out on the street, so the take from that was cut way down to nowhere. Big Sam and I were doing all right with little things, but there wasn't the easy money there was in the hot months. I had a few bucks stashed away under a loose board in the floor at home, but I couldn't see digging it up for some guy I didn't even know.

"Suppose I ain't got twenty bucks?"

"Get it! You don't want to be marked down for a no-good, do you? Suppose it was you in a jam?"

"I ain't getting in no jams."

"You want I should go back and tell my brother that? Maybe you want the cops should start picking on you?"

"I ain't wanting nothing," I told him. "You'll get your twenty bucks. I just wanted to know what the score was, that's all."

So I came up with the money. I was learning. No matter how free and independent you thought you were, there was always somebody higher up to put the squeeze on, and to call the turn. If you didn't have anything, you got pushed around. And the moment you had a nickel and a dime to rub together, there were guys up above demanding a cut of it for this and that.

You had to pay off just for being allowed to make a buck.

I'm fourteen at the time but I don't look it. I'm still under-sized, like I was going to be all my life, and still wearing short pants. Pretty soon I'm going to be able to get my working papers, but the way I see it they are not going to do me much good. I'd already seen the kind of jobs kids my age got when they started out. Working as a helper on a vegetable truck or in the stock room of some sweatshop or stuff like that. Getting yelled at and pushed around by anybody and everybody wanting you should break your neck for a lousy seven, eight dollars a week. Winding up like my old man, who didn't know nothing but the macaroni factory and getting drunk on homemade wine on Sunday.

I tried to tell him when he started in trying to run my life. He had it all settled I was to start working in the macaroni factory.

"I fix it. You don't have to go looking for job. You come work with me."

"Forget it. I'll take care of myself."

"How you take care of yourself? Staying out on streets all night? The police take care of you soon!"

"I'll take care of the cops, too."

But he wouldn't have it that way. He kept yelling about the macaroni factory like it was heaven or something. Finally I got a bellyful.

"Me, I don't want any part of any goddamned factory. You want I should wind up like you?"

"Whatsa matter with me? I'm honest man. No one can say Francesco Mauriello not one honest man."

"And what's that get you? You vote the way Mike Petrucci tells you. You chip in for funerals every time Petrucci says give. You shake in your boots does somebody say Maffia out loud. You're a goddamned slave and don't know it!"

By that time everybody is shouting back and forth, with the old lady yelling the loudest. She screams at me I shouldn't talk to my father that way and then she yells at the old man he should let me alone and I'm a nice son and don't I bring money into the house regular.

"What kind of money?" the old man demanded. "What kind of money he bring home?"

I had an answer to that.

"American money. The kind that puts meat on the table instead of nothing but goddamned spaghetti."

We're not ever going to understand one another, the old man and I. We talk two different languages. He's old-country—still back in some mountain village in Sicily. He was born with too many things over him, like the land-lords and the law and the priests. He still didn't understand that this was a different world— a world in which you didn't have to knuckle down to nobody. He figured he was lucky to have four walls that kept the heat in when winter came and running water and a stinking water closet out in the hallway that was always getting stopped up. Maybe at that it was a palace compared to the broken-down stone hut where he was born in Sicily. I wouldn't know. I wouldn't want to know.

All I knew then was that there was a better way of life than sweating it out in a factory. There were the men we kids looked up to in the neighborhood—men who didn't do any work at all but who had the best of everything. Like Mike Petrucci and Black Tony and Joe the Baker. They wore silk shirts with fancy stripes and imported Borsalino hats and two-toned shoes with real patent leather. They had diamonds the size of rocks and a couple of them had even bought cars—big ones like Locomobiles and Pierce Arrows. Did anyone ask what they did for a living, all you got for an answer was a shrug. Maybe it was the Italian lottery or an in of some kind down in the wholesale produce market or being the neighborhood head man in the olive-oil concession. It didn't matter—the important thing was they had power. What they said went.

There wasn't anything to choose between guys like that and my old man. That was one thing they taught you in school—in America one guy was. as good as the next.

I kept thinking of that every time I tangled up with Cherry Nose. He was old enough now to be out of kid stuff, hanging out with older guys. But like I said, when they were handing out brains his brother got them all. All Cherry Nose knew was to hang onto what he had, which was bossing around guys younger than himself. That and taking a cut on every little thing that passed by, just because he was Mike Petrucci's brother.

It got under my skin having to pay off to him just because he had connections he didn't work for. But for the time being there wasn't anything I could do about it.

Sooner or later, though, I knew there was going to be a showdown.

Maybe he figured it the same way. I know he didn't like the business I worked about the docks. All the time Cherry Nose had been running things it had been the same way—we wop kids never got a chance to use the docks on the East River for swimming in the summer. The trouble was, we was too near to the Gashouse District, with all the Irish kids running things their own way along the water front. There were too many of them, and did any of us Italians show up, they run us off. Were we able to pull a fast sneak and get in the water anyway, they'd grab our clothes and then run us naked through the streets.

Looked like we didn't have a chance.

I did a lot of figuring about it, one way or another, and finally I came up with an idea. Maybe it was because it was late spring and we were collecting from the pushcarts again and having to use a little pressure to bring some new ones into line.

I began to wonder why the same thing can't be worked in a different way.

So I talk it over with Big Sam and the outcome is we round up a bunch of neighborhood kids. Late nights we start drifting over into the Gashouse District, carting rocks and half bricks in our shirt fronts. We bust three plate-glass windows in barrooms the first night, and four or five the next, and a couple after that.

Then I send word to Red Nolan, who heads up the Irish gang, that I've got things to talk over with him. Red is a hefty sixteen-year-old mick bastard who'd rather fight than eat. I'm a little nervous about the whole business, but by this time I've gone too far to stop.

Anyway, I pick the corner where I want to meet Red and I take Big Sam with me and in case anything goes wrong I've already got a dozen of our gang armed with bricks and busted bottles stashed away in stores and areaways nearby.

I wait for about five minutes before Red shows up. He's alone, but I can see three or four of his mob clustered around down at the next corner, waiting in case there's a rumble.

Red came to the point right away.

"What the hell's the idea of wanting to see me? You got something on your mind?"

"Maybe. I hear you got trouble in your neighborhood."

"What kind of trouble?"

I shrugged. "I wouldn't know for sure. The way I hear it, a lot of windows are being busted here and there. Big ones that cost plenty of dough to fix."

Red glared at me, and for a minute it looked like he was figuring to swing. He was a big, pasty-faced mick who had grown too fast for his own good. He had one brother was a cop and another a longshoreman and a third who was studying for the priesthood, so he had an idea he was protected all around, no matter what he did.

"Thanks for tipping me off it's you guinea bastards been doing it. It's about time some wop skulls got cracked for good around here."

I stood my ground. I didn't feel like it but I couldn't help myself. There were too many of my own gang watching from where they were hidden for me to back down. Besides, Big Sam was standing alongside me.

"Why don't you start using your head instead of your fists?" I said. "Why don't you start getting smart?"

He started to blow his top again but I cut in before he could finish. He could stop the trouble without any heads being broken, I told him. All he had to do was form a kind of protective association, like we had in our section, and collect a buck or two a week from the different bars. That way the window smashing would maybe stop, and he'd get a reputation in his district for being a kid that carried some weight and not just a mick bastard fighting for the sake of being tough.

It takes time for him to get the idea. Then he's still suspicious. What do I want out of it? Nothing, I tell him. Just an agreement that we wop kids can use certain of the docks for swimming without being bothered. That's all.

So it's a deal.

It boosts my stock plenty in the neighborhood when the word gets around what has happened. The only one who pulls a face about it is Cherry Nose.

"What's the idea of pulling something like that on your own? Why didn't you come to me first?"

I brushed him off. "For what? You had your chance for five years now and you ain't done nothing."

He didn't like it but he didn't know just what to say. Like always, his mind don't work fast.

"You ought to have talked it over with me. It don't look good, me not knowing about things before they happen."

"Ah, go run some errands for your brother!"

It was clear that Cherry Nose and I weren't ever going to get places together.

It was about then that Black-Tony began taking an interest in me.

Black Tony was one of the older guys in the neighborhood who never did any work that could be noticed but always had plenty of money. He'd been in trouble a couple of times when he was younger, for such things as burglary and armed robbery, but now stuff like that was in the past. He spent the late mornings sitting in a chair in the corner barbershop, two or three hours at a time, and the afternoons in the spaghetti house in the middle of the block. The two places were like his office, almost. He got telephone calls there, and two or three guys were always hanging around him, waiting to go off here or there or wherever he might send them.

At this time he was maybe twenty-seven, twenty-eight years old. He came from somewhere down in the boot of Italy and his skin was real dark, which was where he got his nickname from. He tried to make up for it by getting shaved twice a day and having the barber slap plenty of powder on his chin, but it didn't change things any. He was still Black Tony.

One afternoon when he was out in front of the spaghetti house he beckoned me over. He was working on his nails with a gold penknife and he kept on doing it for a while, as if he didn't have anything else on his mind.

I stood there waiting. Something told me to keep my trap shut. Finally he looked up.

"You act like you got a head on your shoulders, Tony."

I shrugged. Then I said, "Maybe it's because I got the same name as you."

He laughed. "Maybe. How'd you like to make a few bucks doing errands for me?"

"What kind of errands?"

"Delivering stuff." He hesitated and gave me a sharp look and laughed again—a flat, ugly laugh. "Some of my boys can't keep their mind on business, does a fancy dame look like she's ready and waiting. You ain't old enough to have woman trouble yet, are you?"

"You kidding?"

So that was the beginning of that. The packages Black Tony gave me to deliver were no bigger than envelopes, with two or three little folded-over white packets inside. I didn't have to be a mind reader to know what was inside, but it was none of my business. I didn't ask questions. Some things it's better if you don't know too much.

Those errands of Black Tony's took me out of the neighborhood for what was really the first time. It's a funny thing being born in the slums—you don't feel safe and sure and certain of things when you get outside. With a bunch of other kids I'd gone now and then over to Fourteenth Street to the burlesque show and a couple of times as far uptown as the Hippodrome and the Palace. But we just did it to show we could, not because we really wanted. When we got out of our own district we traveled in gangs because we felt more comfortable that way, and we did a lot of shouting and pushing around just to show we were as good as anybody else. Sometimes it took a lot of yelling to make it seem that way.

Now I was on my own when I got outside my home territory. Ever since I'd been making my own money I'd dressed clean and neat. I didn't look like any gutter hoodlum. Even so, my first trips I was always on edge, figuring any minute some strange cop would snarl at me to go on back where I belonged.

The places I got sent to mostly were small theatrical hotels off Broadway, between Herald Square and Forty-second Street, or sometimes an apartment on upper Seventh Avenue. I got me a dummy package of toilet water from the corner drugstore, in case a doorman or somebody got nosy, and stuck the envelope Black Tony gave me down in a bottom fold of my knee pants.

Usually it would be a dame waiting for me, with a bad case of the shakes and looking like she'd been through a couple of wringers. The first time she'd stare at me as though she were seeing the wrong kind of ghost.

"Where's Joe?"

"Joe couldn't come. I brought what you wanted."

"Where is it? Give it to me!"

I'd shake my head. "I was told to get paid first. Ten dollars for this, and twenty on what you owe."

Then the fireworks would start. Worse language than I ever heard any of the girls at Dirty Mamie's cat house using.

"That dirty dago son-of-a-bitch! He promised me if I let him ..." Then they'd stop short and give me a funny look. I'm still undersized, still in knee pants. Even so, once or twice they tried to pull a fast one.

"Look, boy. What's your name?"

I'd say something in Italian. Something dirty, usually.

"What?"

"That's my name."

"Well, look, whatever your name is. You just leave what you've brought and tell Joe I'll fix it up with him next time."

I'd shake my head again. "Joe ain't got nothing to say about this. I take my orders from somebody else."

They'd make a reach for me then. Sometimes they'd just got out of bed and had next to nothing on. They'd let me see it all and start to purr.

"You look like a sweet boy. I'll bet you're real grown-up, too. Do you know what having a good time is?"

"Sure. Going to the baseball games."

They'd give up then and dig down under the mattress or someplace and come up with the ten bucks arid maybe five or six on what they owed. I'd even put up a beef about that, although Black Tony had told me to take whatever I could get on the back account.

Then I'd unbuckle the bottom of one pants leg and fish out the little envelope.

They'd grab it fast, like it was the only thing in the world that mattered, and send me on my way. Once they got what they wanted they couldn't get rid of me quick enough.

They always made me feel disgusted. From then on I never had any use for junkies—they've got no respect for themselves or anybody else. I've had plenty of them working for me in my time, but I never trusted any of them. They'll do anything to get a shot. If it's a woman, she'll lay up with a dog, and a man will frame his own grandmother if he's got the cold sweats and it's the only way he can get what he needs. But the cops like it that way. Give them a phony case where they want to pin a rap on somebody and haven't any evidence and they can always fall back on a couple of junkies to say whatever they want on the witness stand.

Like they did with Lucky.

Sometimes I made deliveries on upper Seventh Avenue. In those days it was still a high-class neighborhood. I got inside some of the apartments, and for the first time I saw how different some folks lived. You didn't step from the hallway right into the kitchen, like at home. You didn't get hit right in the nose with the stink of garlic and peppers and sour wine. Everything wasn't jammed up in a couple of rooms that a breath of fresh air would curl up and die in did it ever get a chance to enter. There was an entrance hall just for waiting in, and off that a big room with maybe a grand piano and the kind of fancy gilt furniture I'd seen before only in moving-picture lobbies. The kind of home where a guy could get off by himself and be private.

Someday, I promised myself, I was going to have a place like that. A dozen rooms all to myself, with a big piano and fancy phonograph and rugs so thick you had to look down to see what you were walking on.

And everything clean. So goddamned clean that even the flies wouldn't dare come in.

I knew what I wanted now. I wanted out of the stinking slums I'd been born in.

CHAPTER THREE

'M SEVENTEEN YEARS OLD when I take a tumble.

That was right at the end of the war, with Prohibition coming up shortly. But in those days we never thought that meant there was going to be a gold mine for everybody. A gold mine with a graveyard right underneath it.

I'm still working for Black Tony and running my own little deals with Big Sam on the side. We're doing a nice business protecting the pushcarts and we've even branched out a little to take in some of the small stores that aren't tied in with any big outfit. We've organized the younger kids that are always sneaking packages off trucks just for the hell of it, and now when they get stuff they bring it to us and Big Sam and I fence it to a couple of places over on Second Avenue. That way everybody makes a penny and things are more businesslike.

Cherry Nose is still in my hair. He's older now, but he hasn't learned anything. Just getting by moving in his brother's shadow, figuring he ought to be a big shot on his brother's name alone.

He didn't like it any because I stopped cutting him in on deals. Once or twice he tried to brace me about it.

"What's the idea of not coming to me no more about things, Tony?"

"For what?"

"My brother says you should."

"You and your brother!" I spat.

I figured that Black Tony was all the protection right then I needed. What I didn't know was that Black Tony and Mike Petrucci were on the outs. It was Maffia business, but I couldn't know that at the time, either.

Just like I couldn't ever swear that somebody put the finger on me. But it was too pat. I was making a delivery for Black Tony one afternoon when the cops picked me up. When they shook me down they came up with the packet of heroin, but I noticed it didn't surprise them any.

In the back room down at the precinct house they start putting the screws on. I keep claiming I don't know from nothing.

"Who gave you this stuff?"

"A guy on the corner give me a buck to deliver it. That's all I know."

A beefy-faced cop in plain clothes backhands me on the side of the head.

"Quit lying! You know Tony Coppola?"

"Nah."

I got belted on both sides of the face then. Back and forth, back and forth.

"Stop lying, you dago punk! You know Coppola! He lives in the same block you do."

"I don't know."

I got a beating like I never got before. I was a lot older before I ever read what a sadist was, and then all I could think about was those goddamned cops. They had their coats off and the sweat was streaming down their faces and they had an animal stink to them. After a while I couldn't feel nothing much any more—you take just so much and then your body goes numb. I couldn't talk if I wanted to, my throat was all clogged up with blood and spit and it hurt to just breathe.

So finally they gave up.

Afterward I lay there in the cell, tasting the salt blood and bile and sick to my stomach. I was so bitter inside it was like fingers tearing at my guts. I swore someday I'd get even—someday I'd get back at every one of those sons-of-bitching cops if it took a lifetime. Someday I'd be able to hand them what they'd given me, and make them like it.

They hauled me downtown in the morning and booked me. Did anyone want to know why I looked like I'd been through a meat grinder, the answer was simple. I'd been beat up resisting arrest.

That's what they alway say. Beat up resisting arrest. He tried to resist an officer, Your Honor, and we was forced to subdue him. That's what the mick bastards always say in their thick brogue.

It's not until I'm slammed in the Tombs that Black Tony's mouthpiece gets to me. Up until then Tony don't know what's happened, although he has an idea when I don't show. I've been picked up in another precinct and kept there overnight before they enter me on the blotter. That's another favorite trick the cops have got. It's not supposed to be that way, but that don't make no matter. Holding you overnight without booking you gives them a chance to work you over, like they did me, and maybe learn something the easy way.

Black Tony's lawyer was a smart Jew from downtown. He didn't waste any time in double talk.

"They've got you booked on a narcotics rap. What kind of story did you tell them?"

"No kind of story. A guy give me a buck to deliver a package. That's all I know."

"That all you told them?"

"I don't know nothing else."

"Did they mention any names? Ask you if you knew different people?"

"They mentioned a lot of names. They didn't mean nothing to me."

"That why they beat you up?"

"Maybe they didn't like my looks."

He told me to take it easy and he'd go fix bail. He gave me a pack of butts and a guard took me back upstairs to the detention cells. Two hours later I got hauled down again and over the bridge to the court and up before a magistrate.

I was out on $2,000 bail.

When we hit the street, Simons, the lawyer, wants to know if I've got cab fare. I remember then.

"Them sons-of-bitches didn't give me back my personal property. I had a watch and over a hundred bucks in cash and some other stuff."

"Don't blow your top. I'll get it back for you." He dug down in his pocket and slipped me a couple of tens. "Don't hunt up Tony right away. He'll get in touch with you."

When I got home the old lady took one look at me and started weeping and wailing and calling on saints that God Himself had forgotten.

"What they do to you, *bambino*? What happened?"

"Nothing. Nothing, Mamma. I had an accident, that's all."

She began rushing around for all kinds of hot oils and rags and I had a hard time making her leave me alone. I just wanted to get by myself and think.

When the old man came home that night it was worse. When he found out that nothing was broken and I was going to live he began storming about my being a bum and hanging out on the street all day and night and the next time I'd come home dead.

Finally I couldn't take any more of it and walked out. I went down and sat on the front steps and sent a kid to find Big Sam. It was ten minutes before he appeared. He took one long look at me and then asked just one question.

"Who done it?"

"No one you can settle for me, Sam. It was the cops."

"The dirty bastards!"

"Sure. I've been calling them names for the past twenty hours. But that don't help none. Look, Sam, I want you should find me a room. A big one. And clean. Maybe there's one over Chico's place."

One thing about Big Sam. He don't never waste time asking a lot of reasons for things. He goes ahead and does what he's told and wonders later.

So that night I moved away from home. It had to come sooner or later, and that time was as good as any. It wasn't the kind of place I'd dreamed about—not the kind of place I'd had in my mind ever since I saw the insides of those apartments on Seventh Avenue—but it was a beginning.

Afterward I made a habit of stopping in the old place every day after the old man had gone off to work. Mamma always had a couple of handkerchiefs freshly washed and ironed for me, and I'd leave five, ten dollars. She never wanted it but I used to tuck it down her neck.

"You keep it, Mamma. Maybe someday you'll need it."

"You good son, Tony."

"Sure. Thanks for the handkerchiefs, Mamma."

"Everything all right, Tony?"

"Sure. Everything's fine."

Once or twice, when I couldn't make it, I'd send Big Sam or somebody.

"Tony sent me for his handkerchiefs."

"He's all right?"

"Yeah. Just busy on some business. He couldn't get here."

"You tell him tomorrow he come for himself."

"Sure. I'll tell him, Mrs. Mauriello."

It was a game, kind of. But we played it right up until the end. Even when I was away, right after, for seven months, I made Black Tony send the money around by Big Sam every day. It made her know that I'd be back soon and everything would be the same.

Black Tony came around to see me the following night. I'd got word to wait for him, but I wasn't figuring to show myself much on the street until my face healed up. He brought my watch and the stuff they'd taken from me at the police station.

I counted the money and started swearing. There was only forty dollars in the roll.

"Them grafting cheap bastards held out more than sixty bucks of my money. I had over a hundred dollars."

"Try to prove it. You're lucky they left you any."

He went for his own roll, peeled off four fifties, and put them on the table.

"The mouthpiece says you didn't tell them nothing downtown."

"That's right."

"They mention my name?"

"A hundred times. Looked like they couldn't think of nothing else."

He began cursing in Italian—a string of mean, ugly curses. It took time to realize it wasn't the cops he was swearing at but somebody else. Mike Petrucci. I stared at him hard.

"I don't get it. Ain't no wop going to finger another wop."

It wasn't exactly that way, he explained. The word had just gone out that he didn't have any more protection in certain quarters. And the cops had been quick to take advantage of it.

I still wanted to know. "What's Petrucci got against you?"

He clammed up a little then. Seems like it was Maffia business and something not to be talked about. But I'd heard enough around and about to know part of the score. Petrucci had ambitions to fill the shoes of Lupo the Wolf Saietta, who had been head of the downtown end of the Maffia and who was being sent up for a long stretch on account of a little counterfeiting trouble. In a way it figured, because Petrucci was in the wholesale produce market and so was Ciro Terranova, the chief of the Maffia in East Harlem and the Bronx. So it looked like Petrucci was in. There were a lot of men who couldn't see it that way, though, and there had been a couple of killings already.

Up to then I'd been too young to take much notice of such things, but now I began to wonder.

One thing was certain. Whoever Black Tony had thrown his lot in with, it hadn't been Mike Petrucci.

I laid low for a while, letting Big Sam do most of the collecting from our little setups, in case any of the cops were tailing me. And it was about a week later that Black Tony came around again with the bad news.

"Simons says he can get the case postponed six months, a year maybe. But they nailed you with the goods, and sooner or later you got to take a bit. I'm sorry, but that's the way things are, kid." He hesitated, looking at me sharply. "He says if you cop a plea he might be able to make a deal."

I'd already thought it over during the week, figuring on the worst. The only safe way to figure.

"O.K. Tell him to hurry it up. I want to get it over quick."

"I won't forget the way you're keeping your mouth shut. You proved yourself once and for all to me, kid."

I said, "That's fine. You can do some proving, too, while I'm away."

"Such as?"

"Pay off Big Sam for me while I'm gone. Ten bucks a day. Five of it goes to my old lady."

"You remember your friends."

"If they remember me."

It was another three weeks before Simons could work it to bring me up before the right kind of judge, and the windup of it was I got sentenced to a year up to the reformatory at New Hampton Farms. The mouthpiece got me aside long enough to tell me he'd have me out in six, seven months on parole and in the meantime not to worry, that everything would be taken care of.

For the record, it took eight months before they sprung me. It's a funny thing about that stretch—I hated it like I never hated anything and swore I'd forget it as soon as I could. I always spit when I think about the place, yet in a strange way I'm glad it happened when it did. I learned a lot of things sooner than I might have otherwise, and got a chance to do some thinking and planning.

In lots of ways the Farms was like the East Side. The same gangs fighting for control of things in the yard and dormitories and cell blocks, the same uniforms to look out for. Only this time they were screws instead of cops, but they added up to just the same. Meaner and more vicious, if anything. There's got to be something wrong about a man to begin with to make him want to put on a uniform and throw his weight around a prison. It's not the money, because they don't get paid enough to keep themselves in socks. The answer is they are born small and mean and without enough brains to make a living in the outside world. Give them a uniform and a blackjack and a bunch of keys to rattle in some prison and they forget for a while they are failures, they get to thinking they're God Almighty. They got men under them to push around who can't answer back and that's all that counts.

And they've got a thousand cute little ways of working off that meanness behind the walls. They can forget to turn on the lights at the end of the day in the dormitories, so that for fifteen, twenty minutes you're sitting in the dark not able to read or do anything. They can shove their goddamned flashlights in your eyes when they are making the midnight count, pretending they couldn't see was it you or a dummy under the covers. They can stand over you in the mess hall, glaring down at you and making sure you eat every bit of slop on your tray even if it stinks so that you lose your appetite if you ever had one. They can haul you up before the main guy for looking at them cross-eyed. If you talk in Italian or some language they can't understand in front of them, that's a rap, too. They figure you must be talking about them and calling them their right names.

Deep down inside they must know what they are.

And all the while you buy them just the way you buy cops on the outside. Only instead of money it's packages of butts and bars of candy they hold you up for. They all come from the same litter of dogs.

The second day there I bumped into Red Nolan. I knew he'd got a bit a few months before, but I hadn't known until then where he had been sent. Seems he'd been hiring out with a bunch of strike-breakers in some labor trouble over in the garment district. He'd been carrying a gun, which is bad for a guy that's hotheaded, and he ended up by killing somebody. What with his brother's connections and one thing and another they were able to get the charge cut down from murder to manslaughter and then were able to pull some more strings to get him sent to the reformatory instead of up the river to the Big House.

He'd been there long enough to know all the connections and to head up the biggest mob in the place. He gave me a hand, but I could see what was in his mind. He was wondering where I was going to fit in.

"How you planning to make it here, Tony?"

I let him know right away. "The easy way. I just want the time to ride by so I can get the hell out. I ain't looking to be no politician around here."

"Maybe I can help you."

"Anything you can put me wise to I'd appreciate."

So that was that. There wasn't any point in tangling with Red behind the walls just to prove who was top man in a dump that didn't count. Besides, too many of the screws were micks themselves. For what it was worth, the odds didn't figure.

Even so, the time went hard. I heard from Big Sam regular. He wrote my old lady's letters for her. According to the records, he was down as my cousin Giuseppe. What the screws up front that handled the mail and censored the letters didn't know they couldn't wonder about or pass the information back to the cops in the city. You learn quick not to trust nothing or no one.

Big Sam had ways of letting me know how things were going outside. "I see our big cousin Tony the other day," he would write. "He comes around regular about every week. He is good about helping with money at home while you are away."

That way I would know that Black Tony was coming up with the scratch he'd promised every week.

Then Big Sam would write, "I still got the pushcart business but some folks is poor pay. I wish you were back here to help out as in times past. You know how to handle certain people. But there is still money coming in though not enough to make anybody rich."

And I could see that Big Sam wasn't doing so good on the collecting end from the pushcarts and small stores. But he was trying, and that was all that counted.

Once he wrote, "I was by Aunt Mamie's on the next block the other day and she and all her daughters was sorry to hear what happened to you. She said when you come home you should have one on the house. Ha. Ha. Maybe I should take care of this for you."

I knew from that that he had been around to Dirty Mamie's, although we had given up the kid stuff of running errands for them long ago. But Big Sam could never keep away from women. That was his one weakness.

Like I say, I got a chance to do a lot of thinking. From the time I'd been old enough to wipe my own nose I'd been scheming and conniving and taking chances just to get by and make an extra buck or two. And where had it got me? I only had to look around to see the answer.

I was sitting in the sun in the corner of the yard one afternoon, dragging on a cigarette and turning things over in my mind, when Red drifted up and flopped down. We passed a word or two and then I come out with what I'd been mulling over.

"You know something, Red? We think we're smart guys, but we're not. We're just goddamned suckers."

"You talking about yourself?"

"Both of us. Figure it out. Since we've been kids we've been doing the same thing. Fighting and knocking our brains out, and for what? I'll tell you. Except for little stuff, we've. mostly been doing the dirty work and some guy higher up that we don't even see or know anything about maybe has been getting the gravy."

"Nobody ever made much from me."

"Don't kid yourself. What you and I and a lot of guys like us kick in all adds up. Some guy somewhere sitting back and pulling strings and making the right connections is doing all right by himself. Take yourself. How much was you making doing somebody's dirty work strike-breaking?"

Red shrugged. "Ten bucks a day, and it was easy money."

"Is this bit you're doing easy? That came along with the ten bucks, though I'll bet they didn't tell you so at the time. Ten bucks they paid you for going out and busting heads and maybe getting your own busted. They weren't giving you nothing. Someone higher up was getting a hundred times that much."

"So what can we do about it?"

"I don't know," I admitted. "But someday I'll find an angle. I ain't aiming to be a stooge all my life. It's just a matter of thinking things out. Like this strike business. Some Union mug steams a lot of guys into walking out on the job because they ain't getting paid enough, and then the son-of-a-bitch that owns the factory starts hiring goon squads to beat up the workers. All kinds of simple guys getting the hell beat out of them because one man says go and another man says no. There ought to be an in-between, like when you and I settled things so us wops could go swimming off the docks without no heads being busted."

"They're after my brother who works on the docks to join up with a union. He ain't doing it. He don't like having to quit work any time a union boss tells him."

I began to get the shape of an idea.

"You ought to join a union when you get out, Red. You got a way with your own people. I bet it wouldn't be any time until you was a boss of some kind."

"You crazy?"

I didn't answer right away. There wasn't any point in it. Not then. But I had a funny feeling about the future—almost as though I could see into it. And I could see me and Red doing business of some kind. I didn't know just what, but it was there.

After that I began watching him more carefully, studying him and trying to figure the way his mind worked and how he handled himself. And I made a point of being friends.

He was still at the Farms when I left. He hadn't been getting more than a buck now and then from home, and I promised to send him some regular in his brother's name. An investment, kind of.

I got back into town just three hours after Black Tony's body had been picked up in an alley off Mulberry Street with five bullets in it.

It was the same night that I was braced to do my first murder.

CHAPTER FOUR

DIDN'T go right home when I got back to the city. I had certain things to straighten out and plans to make, and I knew that as soon as my old lady saw me that would be the end of everything for about forty-eight hours. First there would be a lot of weeping with her asking me a hundred times was I all right and crying that I looked like they had starved me and then there would be the kind of feast that only Italians can cook up, with everything taking nineteen hours to make and twice as long to eat. All the relatives and every friend the family had would come trooping in to shake your hand and drink a toast, and it would be like fourteen saints' days rolled into one. In our neighborhood when a guy came home from jail he always got that kind of celebration, the best the family could afford. It was kind of a tradition.

But I had matters I wanted to attend to first. I wanted the low-down on what had been happening since I went away.

I'd sent a kite out of New Hampton a week before to Big Sam, letting him know what day and time I was due back and telling him to be waiting for me in the back room of Luigi's spaghetti house.

He was there, eating a big plate of ravioli and washing it down with red wine when I came in. I spoke his name before he saw me and he jumped up so quick he half knocked the table over and the wine went slopping over everything.

I grinned at him. "Take it easy, Sam. I ain't no cop."

"Tony! Jesus Christ, Tony, it's good to have you back."

"It's good to be back."

I sat down and ordered up some food. Then Luigi came in and shook hands and slapped me on the back and said whatever I should want was on the house and to take things easy. When he went back into the kitchen I poured out a little bit of Sam's wine into a glass and filled it up with water. I like the taste of wine but I made a point of never taking much. Not when I had things on my mind. I seen too many smart guys let a bottle do the thinking for them and find out too late that the thinking was all wrong.

I started asking Sam how things were and I could see right away he had some kind of news he didn't quite know how to tell. So in the beginning he started off with little things, like the take from the pushcarts and small stores and stuff like that.

"I got your end of it right here." He reached in his pants pocket and pulled out a roll. "I kept figures on everything, including what Black Tony gave me." He hesitated and gave me an awkward look. "It ain't all here. I mean, I used a little more than I should for personal matters. But I kept track so you can get it back."

"What was her name?"

"I didn't say nothing about no dame."

I reached over and clapped him on the shoulder. "You didn't need to, Sam. Food and some broad are the only two things you'd ever spend extra dough on." I put the roll of money into my pocket without counting it. "How about the room? Were you able to get my old place back?"

"I got one just as good. In the next block."

"So what else is new?"

Again he gave me a funny look. "You seen the papers yet today?"

"Why?"

"I thought maybe you'd read about Black Tony. But I guess they haven't had time to print it."

I gave him a hard look. "All right. Hurry it up. What are you trying to tell me?"

"He got it last night sometime. They found his body this morning over near Mulberry."

Coming like that it hit me for a minute. A lot of the plans I'd been making while I was away were built around some of the money I'd figured I would be making from Black Tony. I'd even had it in mind to brace him for enough to start me off on my own on a deal I'd been mapping out.

Now all of a sudden everything was changed.

"Who done it?"

"The cops ain't picked up nobody yet."

"To hell with the cops. What's the word going around?"

Big Sam began acting uncomfortable again. "Nobody ain't wanting to say. There's been a lot of funny business while you was away. Important guys getting killed. It's inside stuff—a kind of family fight. Nobody asks any questions, and if they do they don't get no answer."

I had a feeling what it was then. A family fight meant Maffia business. I remembered the way Black Tony had cursed the name of Petrucci after I had taken my pinch. It looked like it wasn't settled yet who would step into Lupo Saietta's shoes. The side Black Tony had been on must be carrying some weight or they wouldn't have had to rub him out.

While I'm turning these things over in my mind Big Sam speaks up again.

"There's someone wanted to make a meet with you for this afternoon."

"I ain't seeing nobody until I get straightened out." Then something struck me. "How'd anyone know I'd be here today? I didn't write no one but you."

"I told Black Tony."

"But he ain't here no more."

"The party he was connected with is."

I noticed then how Big Sam kept looking at his watch and then at the door, like he was expecting someone any minute. I half got out of my chair.

"What the hell goes on? You shouldn't make no meets without telling me first, Sam. Maybe it's a setup."

"Jesus, Tony! I didn't have nothing to say about it. The guy just told me flat he'd be here. It was Lucania, from up on Fourteenth Street."

"Salvatore?"

Big Sam nodded.

I knew him, the way you know everybody from around about that gets into trouble. Salvatore had finished a short rap up at New Hampton the year before for narcotics. I'd heard his name a lot while I was up there and the grapevine had it that he had made the right connections and was heading places.

I hadn't known he and Black Tony were tied in together on any deals. If they had been, and he was taking over, maybe he figured on me working for him, and I wasn't sure I wanted it that way.

While I was still trying to decide what was what, he came in. In those days he wasn't bad-looking—his face hadn't been cut and scarred up the way it was later. But he had a tough, hard look about him even though his voice was soft.

He started talking in Italian, in the same Sicilian dialect my folks used. "Welcome home, Tony."

"Thanks."

He looked at Sam then and jerked his head toward the outside. "Go take a little walk for yourself. Come back in ten, fifteen minutes."

Big Sam started to get up and I cut in quick.

"Wait a minute. Big Sam's with me. He ain't taking a walk nowhere without I say so."

Lucania sat down. His eyes didn't have any expression as he stared at me.

"Black Tony said you were smart. Said you used your head and kept your mouth shut."

I kept quiet.

"He liked you a lot. He had plans for you."

"He ain't here now. So what plans he had don't count."

Lucania took his time about answering, like he was feeling his way which words to use.

"That's for you to decide. He talked to certain parties about you." He stopped, looked at Sam and then back at me. "He wasn't a Sicilian, like you and me, but right now that don't matter. You understand, I ain't talking for myself. I got a message for you from some other people."

I sat quiet for a moment. Then I made up my mind to play it through.

"Go sit at another table, Sam." When he was over to the other side of the room I turned back to Lucania. "All right. I'm listening."

He came to the point quick enough, but without saying too much. Either I was smart enough to understand, or I wasn't. Did he need to draw a diagram, then he would go back and tell the people who had sent him that maybe I was all right for little things but that was all. It was up to me to see beyond the words he was using.

He said straight out that the man he was working for was going to take Saietta's place as head of the downtown and Brooklyn end of the Maffia. Only he didn't say Maffia—he called it the family.

"My man's going to head up this branch of the family. But there's two or three people got the same ambition, and they've been making trouble. The kind of trouble that came Black Tony's way."

"So?"

"Tony didn't have any partners. There's no one to take over what he was doing. Unless you wanted to even up the score and get the party that ordered him killed. That might mean a lot to you, should things work out right."

I knew what he was suggesting. I should go out with a gun and get the party that ordered Tony's murder. But it was more than that. They had plenty of men handy to do that kind of killing—they didn't need me for that. What was happening, they were offering me a chance to join the family. That was the way it worked in those days. You did a killing on order and you were in. Always after that you had family protection and family connections. How far you went was up to you, but you would always have something to do, some way of making an easy buck.

I said carefully, "Suppose I wanted to even the score. Who would I get?"

"Someone right in your neighborhood. The biggest one you can think of."

"Petrucci?"

"That's right."

It was a funny sensation. Always Mike Petrucci had been looked up to and feared like God Himself in our district. In a way you'd sooner even think of knocking off a cop. You'd figure it would be safer.

But playing safe wouldn't get you nowhere. Once in a while you had to take a gamble, at least when you were starting out. And I needed some help and connections for what I had in mind.

Even so, it wouldn't be easy.

"He's got friends and relatives all over the neighborhood. Did anything happen to him here, whoever done it wouldn't last two minutes."

That end of it had been thought out, Lucania told me. On Thursday nights Petrucci could always be found in the back room of a wine house on Bleecker Street, playing cards with a couple of old *paisanos* and seeing runners for the Italian lottery. It was a place where he wouldn't ever expect any trouble and a section where I wasn't known by sight.

"Thursday," I said. "That's tomorrow night. My folks will be giving me a feast then with a houseful of people."

"So you've got yourself an alibi. You won't be missed for half an hour or so."

"I'll need a gun."

"I brought one."

He had it wrapped up in a handkerchief in his inside pocket. He had something else for me. Five century notes.

"Black Tony would want you to have this. You need expense money for clothes and things your first days back in town."

He yelled for Luigi then and ordered some more wine. Big Sam came back over to the table. I just touched the wine to my lips when it was poured out. I was anxious for Lucania to get the hell on his way.

I wanted to be alone with my thoughts and to get things straightened out in my mind.

I went down to Canal Street with Big Sam and bought a blue suit and some white shirts and socks and underclothes. I bought Sam a suit, too, but I couldn't change his mind about getting something in fancy stripes and a silk shirt that looked like it was patterned after a barber pole. But that was the way Big Sam always liked things. Did he get something new, he wanted it different, so everybody would know. Even women.

Afterward we went to the room Big Sam had found for me and I took a bath and shaved and put on the clean new things I had bought. They felt good. Someday, I promised myself, I was going to have closets full of nothing but clean, crisp clothes— so new they were like they just came from the store. I wouldn't never have to put on anything old or used unless I wanted to. Not the same thing day after day, month after month, like when I was growing up in the streets before I got smart.

Finally I got fixed up and went home. It was just like I'd known it would be. The old lady started crying and throwing her arms around me and crying some more and then deciding that they had starved me to death.

"I ain't hungry, Mamma. Honest."

"They feed you good macaroni and *pasta fagiuli* like I make while you were gone?"

"No."

"Then you didn't eat right. They starve you. Now your mamma fix it you eat good."

It was late afternoon and she made me sit in the kitchen while she started making meat sauce and crying why didn't I let her know before so she would have time to cook things. But tomorrow would be different. Tomorrow we would have a feast.

"You stay home now, Tony, eh? You not going to get into no more trouble."

"No, Mamma," I said. "I won't get into trouble no more."

The old man came home then. He swore at me for a no-good and then put his arms around me and kissed me on both cheeks and then said maybe now I'd learned I didn't know everything.

"That's right, Papa. There's a lot I don't know."

Big Sam came in then. I'd told him to wait out on the street until he saw the old man come home. He'd brought what I told him to. He acted like he hadn't seen me before and shook hands and welcomed me home. Then he put the two packages on the table.

"I brought you a present, Tony."

I opened them up. There was the box of twisted Italian cigars and the bottle of real brandy I had bought earlier. Then Sam went into the kitchen to speak to the old lady and I shook my head at Papa.

"Sam's another one who don't know everything. He didn't remember I don't smoke cigars or drink much. You'll have to use them up for me so he won't feel bad."

That way the old man didn't mind taking the brandy and cigars. It wasn't like a present he'd have to thank me for. He wouldn't have to ask where the money came from for me to buy stuff my first day home.

After he got a drink in his hand and a smoke in his face I knew he would be quiet for a while.

From then on it was just the way I'd known it would be. That night was quiet, but the next day, starting early in the afternoon, all the neighborhood began dropping in.

The eating started then and kept on going with different people in and out of the place all the time. The place was so crowded that did I want to talk private to some guy that had been in my gang when we was kids, I had to take him out in the hall, pretending like we was using the water closet.

I kept watching the clock, and when it was quarter past nine I eased out and down the stairs. Should anyone see me, I had it ready that I was going after more wine.

Big Sam was waiting for me over in my room. I took the gun that Lucania had given me from under a loose board Sam had fixed in the closet. I checked it to make sure it worked right and then slid it in my pants pocket. It felt heavy and hard against my leg when I walked.

"You got your gun, Sam?"

"Like you told me."

"All right. Let's go."

He hadn't even asked what was up. He didn't ask any questions now as we walked over to West Broadway and then up to Bleecker Street. We walked two doors down from the corner of Sullivan and I motioned Sam into the doorway of a hardware store that was closed for the night. Right across the street was the wine shop.

"I've got an errand over there, Sam. If there's trouble when I come out, cover me up."

"Want I should go in with you?"

"No. This is private business."

I went across the street and opened the door of the wine shop. No one was in front and I walked on back through some hanging curtains.

Mike Petrucci and three other old-timers were sitting at a table playing cards. Petrucci looked up and frowned at me. He wasn't sure maybe that he recognized me. As far as he was concerned, I was just a neighborhood kid that had come up too fast.

Somebody said, "What you want here, kid?"

"I got a message for Mike Petrucci."

"Who sent you?"

"Black Tony."

Petrucci started to push back his chair. "What you mean, that son-of-a-bitch sent you? He can't send—"

I didn't wait. I had the gun out of my pocket. I was standing across the table from him and I squeezed the trigger four times. I could see his chest kind of jump when they hit home.

I left some shots in the gun in case anything happened when I hit the street, but nothing did. Big Sam was waiting for me, right where I had left him, and he tailed after me as I headed up to Fourth Street and then east toward Second Avenue.

When we reached the mouth of a dark alley I stepped into it and wiped off the gun carefully and wrapped it up in a handkerchief. I gave it to Big Sam and told him to go over to the West Side and ditch it in the washroom of any cheap lunchroom. Some mick punk would likely pick it up, and after that if it ever fell into the hands of the cops they wouldn't be able to tell from nothing when they started checking the bullet markings. I'd been reading about such things and figured it was smarter that way than dropping it in the river.

When I got back to the house I had been gone just thirty-five minutes. The old lady was the only one who had noticed I wasn't around.

"Where was you, Tony? Don't you see your godfather when he come in?"

"I was in the toilet upstairs."

"Everybody so happy to see you back. You be a good boy from now on, eh, Tony?"

"Sure, Mamma," I said. "Sure. I'll always be a good boy. You don't have to worry about me."

CHAPTER FIVE

I T WAS all in my mind what I wanted to do, and now the way was open to me was I smart enough to operate right. It was Prohibition and everybody all over town was making a quick buck peddling alcohol could they get it.

I'd figured a way to make it a business and to do myself good in other ways at the same time.

That's what I told Lucania when we met the day after Mike Petrucci's funeral. It was the biggest one we'd ever had in the neighborhood with everybody turning out to go to the church. There was more flowers than I'd ever seen before in one place. I sent a big wreath myself that cost over a hundred dollars and that I went personal all the way over to a fancy joint on Sixth Avenue to order.

It paid to be respectful in things like that.

The biggest wreath of all was from Joe "The Boss" Masseria. He was a big shot over in Brooklyn and I wondered a little. It ought to have been clear to me then that he was the one who ordered Petrucci rubbed out.

Lucania had it in mind that maybe all I wanted was to take over Black Tony's old business. I told him different.

"I ain't figuring to spend the rest of my life hanging out in front of a barbershop, trying to keep a bunch of junkies in line."

"Somebody has got to handle the business. Black Tony did all right for himself."

So one of my boys could do the same thing, I told him. The business would be taken care of all right, but it wasn't enough. I wanted something else.

"Like what?"

"Like a go-ahead for organizing a little business in my neighborhood. Right now there's all kinds of slop all over town they call alky, with everybody and his grandfather making it a different way. I got an idea. All I need is for the word to go around people should do business with me and maybe the loan of a couple of grand to get started."

What I planned was a string of kitchen stills—one in every house in the neighborhood. Small ones that wouldn't be no loss if they blew up or got knocked off. The kind that could turn out ten, fifteen gallons of alcohol a week without no trouble. That way every wop family in the district would be making a few extra bucks besides what they stole to drink themselves. And with maybe a hundred stills scattered around, I would have myself a thousand gallons of alcohol a week to peddle.

Lucania got the idea. "You could do all right."

"I wouldn't get so much out of it personal," I told him. "I got a lot of boys to take care of. Kids I grew up with. They look to me to keep them busy with one thing and another."

That was one thing I'd already learned. It was the same when you grew up as when you were small. The other guys figured your power by the number you had in your mob. A leader wasn't no bigger than the outfit he had.

So the meeting wound up with Lucania saying he would talk it over with the right parties and let me know and in the meantime I should see about Black Tony's business being taken care of.

A couple of days later he made a meet with me again and told me what I had in mind was O.K., and it was a deal.

❖   ❖   ❖

A week later the mob gave a special blowout for me. They didn't call it that. According to the story Lucania gives me, it's just a kind of friendly little get-together.

"Some of the top boys are throwing a party tomorrow night. You got a special invite."

"What kind of party?"

"No business. Just a chance to break loose among friends."

I thought it over and nodded.

"O.K. Big Sam and me will be there."

I wanted it understood from the start that where I went Big Sam went. That was the way it always had been and that was the way it was always going to be.

They give the affair in the private dining rooms over a wop restaurant in Greenwich Village. It starts off with a kind of banquet at which there is just guys. Important guys, big shots that I hadn't known except by hearsay before, like Johnny Torrio and Joe "The Boss" Masseria and Little Augie. There was ward bosses and a couple of judges and the kind of politicians that is always anxious to show they ain't forgetting where their power comes from.

Lucania introduced me around to this one and that one. "This is the boy I been talking about. He's all right."

I got clapped on the back like I was a long-lost brother by men who would have passed me on the street the day before without giving me a second look.

"Been wanting to meet you, Tony. This is a pleasure."

"Likewise," I said. "Likewise."

But all the time I could see they was watching me. I begin to get the angle. They was wanting to know how I stacked up when I was out of my own district—did I get important too quick or was

I loose-mouthed at the wrong time. That was one of the reasons for all the big hellos and all the drinks being shoved at me.

I took a quick sneak out to the can as soon as I could and grabbed off a waiter in the hallway and made him bring me a shot glass full of olive oil. I downed it in one gulp. Did it do nothing else it would put a lining in my stomach so that what booze I had to take wouldn't hit me too quick. And I got Big Sam off to one side alone.

"This is one of those times you don't know from nothing. Does anyone ask you questions, you tell them I'm the only one who knows the answers."

He looked at me hurt. "Jesus, Tony, I ain't said nothing."

"Keep going the same way. Use your mouth for eating and drinking and not for words."

The guy sitting across from me is a big wop from up in East Harlem. I know he's right or he wouldn't be there. Even so, it gave me a funny feeling when he brought up Mike Petrucci's name, talking loud to me across the table so everybody could hear.

"Somebody did your district a big favor when they rubbed out Petrucci. It must have been a guy with the right kind of guts. You got any ideas about it, Tony?"

I made my eyes blank and finished chewing on a piece of steak before I answered.

"I wouldn't know. Me, I was as surprised as anybody. He never did me no harm personal, you understand." I had a feeling a lot of people were listening so I cut it short. "I guess he must have made a mistake somewhere along the line. The kind you don't make but once."

The big man said, "I'd like to shake hands with the one who did it."

I let myself smile a little.

"I'll pass the word around. But I got a feeling the guy who did it ain't after no credit."

That was during the eating part of the blowout. The dinner was about three-quarters finished when the dames started showing. The kind I'd only seen at a distance before. Show girls from Broadway and fancy women who looked like they were too high-priced to even spit on anybody from the slums. They come in all tricked out like a million dollars, acting so goddamned refined you'd think they was born that way.

Only it didn't last that way long.

What I got a feeling of that night I seen all through the years to come. Guys that come up like I did was always talking and dreaming about the time when they would have dough enough to get whatever dame they wanted and as many as they wanted. Yet when the time came it wasn't never the way they thought it would be. They knew that no matter how rich the women was dressed or how fancy they acted, they was still nothing but god-damned tramps. Tramps they was getting just because they had the right kind of money to throw around.

They bought them and they paid for them, but deep down inside they hated them. It came out in the way they treated them—like dogs they had bought just to show off their fancy tricks.

Cheech, the big guy from up in East Harlem, had a real ladylike-looking blonde alongside him. Her hair was all fixed in careful waves and she had the kind of cool, high-toned voice clerks in Fifth Avenue stores used. She kept trying to make him behave like what she called a gentleman.

"Now, Cheech! You're getting my new evening dress all mussed."

"So who bought it?"

"You did, darling. Don't you like it?"

"No. Take it off and throw it away. I'll get you another."

"Now, Cheech ..."

"Goddamn it, I said take it off!"

He wrestled her around and began pawing away at the dress while she screamed and tried to cover herself up. Everybody started shouting and yelling, like they was at a prize fight, cheering for both sides even though they knew the fight was in the bag. She had on a silk slip and silk and lace pants under the dress and somebody yelled at Cheech wanting to know who had paid for them.

"I did, goddamn it. I paid for everything. It's all mine!"

I couldn't tell whether she was sobbing or just trying to catch her breath from struggling and fighting. It didn't make no difference. Her hair wasn't in neat waves no more and her voice wasn't cool and smooth the way it had been at first.

"You dirty bastard! Why don't you take my shoes and stockings too!"

She was standing up, crying down at him, not trying to cover her nakedness no more.

Cheech laughed at her. "Whores always wear stockings. You ought to know that."

"Don't call me a whore!"

He didn't bother to answer. Just laughed again and pulled her down on his lap and started shoving a slug of whisky down her throat, liking the way she squirmed.

It was like a signal for the other guys to start acting the same way. Girls were squealing and running all over the place, some with their clothes half off and others with nothing on. I could see Big Sam's eyes bugging out.

Sam had been paired off with a big redhead who had come in all wrapped up in furs and a lot of talk about being in the Follies. It was the first time he'd ever been that close to a real show girl except for once when he picked out a drunken broad from the second line of the chorus at the People's. Burlesque over on the Bowery. She was teasing him along, the way bitches always do, and I was afraid any minute he'd get impatient and knock her cold. That was Big Sam—whatever he was after he always tried to get the quickest way. He never wasted no time on fancy frills.

Maybe it would have been all right if he'd done it. There was plenty of other rough stuff going on without nobody paying it no mind. But Big Sam was part of me and I wasn't for having him make a show of himself. I give him the nod to one side.

"Go on over to the Central and hire a suite of rooms."

"You mean I should leave now, Tony? Just when things are getting good?"

"Take the goddamned dame with you."

"Aw,—Tony—"

"You heard me."

The broad put up an argument, the kind that needed only half a century note to settle. I breathed a little easier after she and Big Sam were gone. Now I only had myself to handle.

There was a little number with a baby face and wise eyes that had latched onto me from the start. Everything about her spelled money. First off I figured she must belong to one of the big shots there and I played it easy. But she wasn't for having it that way.

"What's the matter, Tony? Don't you like me?"

"Sure I like you. But I ain't for cutting in on nobody."

"I don't belong to anybody here. Right now I'm a lone wolf."

"So why me?"

She had an answer to that. She had an answer to everything. "I like men who are smart. Men who know where they want to go and how to get there." She spoke her words slow, her eyes on me all the time she was talking as if to make sure I wasn't missing anything. "Smart men need smart women, Tony. Maybe that's one reason I'm with you right now."

I said, "Uh-huh."

I happened to look up then and seen Lucania standing nearby watching me. He gave me a big grin and called out, "Enjoy yourself, Tony. You got some good times coming to you."

"I can wait."

"You don't have to wait for nothing. Gloria will take care of you." He moved closer and gave her shoulder a heavy pat. "You don't have to worry about her none. You can trust her all the way."

I nodded like I was glad to know it.

But all the time I had other things on my mind. Maybe it would have been different if it wasn't the first time I was out with big shots. Then I could have let myself go. But the way things were, I wasn't sure of nothing. And I always liked to see things clear and way ahead.

I begin to feel my head going around from the drinks I had downed and the room was getting hotter all the time. Seemed like everywhere I looked there was nothing but naked broads yelling and dancing or loving some guy up.

Gloria knew how to work on a guy smooth. She didn't come out with nothing rough or crude, but she let you know just the way she looked at you that she was ready and waiting.

All of a sudden I made up my mind.

"Come on, baby. Let's get going."

"Where?"

"What difference does it make?"

"None." She gave me one of her long, steady looks. "None at all, Tony. Not as long as I'm with you."

We got a cab outside and headed over to the Central. She was close up beside me on the seat and the air was full of the stink of hundred-dollar perfume.

"Are you always so quiet, Tony?"

"When I'm thinking."

"Do you have to think now?"

"Sure." I gave her a laugh. "You're enough to start any man thinking."

At the hotel I took her up to the suite I had sent Big Sam over to get. I see his hat and coat and a dame's fur coat dumped careless on a chair in the sitting room. The door to one of the two bedrooms was closed, but. I could hear sounds on the other side. Gloria wanted to know who was in there and I told her it was my sidekick.

"Oh! The big fellow. Sam. Helen must be with him, then."

"If that's her name." She was smart, all right. She knew everything. She knew too much.

My mind was working all the while I watched her take her clothes off. She did it neat and graceful, not in a hurry and not too slow, almost like it was an act she was doing on the stage. And all the time she was talking—talking smooth and easy about all the good times we was going to have together.

"Yeah," I said. "Sure. That's right."

So what am I doing here, I asked myself, fixing to make myself a sucker? I ain't no place yet, I'm just beginning to get a break, and before I even get started I should tie myself up with a wise bitch on the make?

She was proud of her body and she had a right to be. Her skin was as smooth as silk and her breasts full and firm. She ran her hands over them and then down over her waist and hips as if calling my attention to everything.

She came and leaned over me where I was sitting in a chair, her bare body so close to my face that I couldn't turn my head without touching it, and began running her fingers through my hair.

"Relax, Tony. Forget whatever you're thinking about and let yourself go."

So how do I know how close she is to Lucania or one of the other big guys, I asked myself. Maybe there is a reason for all this—maybe they want a tail on me for my private life as well as what business I do. A dame that sleeps with you steady gets to know too much about you, and that ain't never healthy.

She had her lips against my cheek and her fingers were working on my clothes.

"What are you waiting for, Tony? If you're too tired, why don't you rest a while?"

I shook my head, making up my mind at last.

"I ain't tired. I'm just trying to figure how far to trust a dame like you."

She don't act hurt or insulted. She answered like I had a right to ask. Answered too quick.

"All the way, Tony. Try me and see."

"Meaning what?"

"Anything you say. Any time. You'll never have to tell me twice."

I slid her off my lap and got up. "O.K., sister, you wrote the ticket." I took her by the arm and walked over to the bedroom door that was closed and opened it. Big Sam half jumped out of the bed and the redhead with him sat up and started swearing.

"What the hell's the idea of busting in here?"

I didn't pay her no mind. I pulled Gloria in front of me and gave her a hard shove so that she wound up half across the bed.

"Here's another one for you, Sam. Have yourself a real time while you're about it."

She twisted about on the bed to face me, her eyes hard and mean.

"You goddamned bastard! What do you think I am?"

I gave her her own answer. "A wise bitch that don't need to be told nothing twice. Remember? That's the line you give me a minute ago. Go on and prove it!"

I closed the door on her dirty words and picked up my hat and went on out. Maybe everything was on the up and up, maybe I was tossing a good bet out of the window just because I was playing things too careful. But I didn't have no time to take chances on high-class whores, even if I had a mind to.

I had other things to do.

CHAPTER SIX

I T TOOK TIME to get the stills lined up and placed and working. First off I had to hunt up a wop tinsmith who could do what I wanted and then I had to find a wholesale kitchen-supply house and make a deal on a bunch of copper kettles. Then Big Sam and I cornered a rock-headed Neapolitan that had been starving to death in his hole-in-the-wall grocery in our block for twenty years. He was the uncle of Little Cheech, one of the kids in our old mob, and we figured to give him a break.

"You want to start making some money for a change?"

"Why you ask fool questions?"

"O.K., you got partners now. Big Sam and me. We'll fix the papers tomorrow. But we start now. Call up and order twenty hundred-pound bags of sugar."

"You crazy!"

"We'll worry about that. We pay cash for the sugar when it comes. You sell it to people we send in. Same with everything else. From now on Big Sam here will tell you what to do."

It didn't mean too much in the way of money, but the way I looked at it, there wasn't any point in letting outsiders make a profit.

The stills averaged me a hundred apiece. I rented them to the different families for two bucks a week. I told them where to buy the sugar and other stuff for the mash and made them give me receipts showing they had done as I told them. That way I could keep a check that everybody was using the same stuff and the alky would be about the same grade. I sold them the five-gallon tins to put the runoff in, and my own boys, operating under Big Sam, did the collecting.

There wasn't any trouble selling. Speakeasies and kitchen barrooms were springing up all over town, with most of the joints making their own gin and bar whisky and cutting what honest stuff they could get hold of.

In those early days of Prohibition it was nothing but a god-damned madhouse, with no kind of organization at all. New gangs nobody ever heard of before began coming up and throwing their weight around. From the Jew section down around Grand Street a kid named Jack Diamond started getting fancy ideas he was a second Monk Eastman or something, and over on the West Side in the Chelsea district a limey called Owney Madden was all of a sudden a big shot. Up in East Harlem the wops were having trouble with a squarehead who called himself Dutch Schultz, and every other place you turned there was some other new mob.

For a while we had to work hard just to hold our own territory, let alone do any spreading out. In a way it was like the gang fights we used to have as kids, with the micks and the Jews against us wops. And in a way the odds was against us. Like most of the cops had been micks when we was kids, so was most of the law when it came to a showdown on buying graft and protection. What the Irish didn't control in the way of politics, the Jews did. The district leader in our ward was an Italian, but he took his orders from Tammany Hall and wasn't worth nothing in straightening out any trouble. Did one of my boys take a pinch, I had to go elsewhere to arrange a fix.

Looked like we Italians were just getting the leavings.

When it came to keeping any of the new mobs from trying to cut in on our business we didn't get no help at all. We had to settle things our own way.

That is something nobody ever seems to understand. I've been reading all my life, and the way they write about the underworld you'd think it was something all shut off by itself, where they go to knocking off one another just because they don't know no better. Where they are tough just because they like being that way.

You'd think the underworld lived off itself.

Only that's not the picture. What happens is that you've got a business of some kind and you've got to protect it. Like it was in bootlegging, and afterward in the gambling and labor rackets. It takes a lot of time and trouble and money to build up the kind of organization that can give the kind of service the public wants. Then when you've got things operating smoothly, what are you supposed to do when some other mob tries to chisel in, stealing your ideas and your customers?

What they call a legitimate businessman in a fix like that can go to all kinds of courts with all kinds of lawyers, but that is out if what you are doing is supposed to be illegal. Maybe you've been paying everybody from the police commissioner down, but that don't get you anywhere when you need protection against some other mob—a mob that is likely paying off the same as you are.

When that happens you got to go out and settle things your own way—with a baseball bat and a gun.

It's just a matter of business. It ain't got anything to do with the kind of crime they are always writing about in newspapers.

And always you've got worries. I had about a dozen guys in my outfit and maybe twice as many I could call on for anything extra I wanted done. Most of them were good boys but only one or two could be depended on if they had to do their own thinking. So always I had to be on hand to straighten out any rumpus that came up. Big Sam was all right on routine matters and following out orders. Tell him to go beat somebody up and he'd do it without batting an eye. But did he have a decision to make on his own, he'd get in a stew and wind up coming to me.

A nice guy, but no confidence in himself.

Before long there was plenty of money coming in. I read a newspaper story about myself once at the time Dewey was making a name for himself busting up the rackets, and it said that when I wasn't much more than twenty-one I was grabbing off a hundred grand a year in the alky racket. They made it sound like I was rolling in dough.

Only it never was that way. Take those first years after I got my break and started in business. I was handling maybe a thousand gallons of alcohol a week, averaging a buck and a half a gallon profit. That was fifteen C notes. By then I had the Italian lottery for our district and I collected maybe another half grand a week from that. I'd put Joie the Bug to work handling Black Tony's junkie business and he'd turn over a couple grand a month to me after taking his cut. But I had to kick half of that back up the line to Lucania and the men over him. And what was left wasn't clear profit, either. The Bug was a guy who liked to dress flashy and hang out in night clubs and make a splash gambling. Result was he was always getting in some kind of swindle he needed help in and half the time he was in hock to me.

The alky dough was the same. It came in to me, but I had to pay it out. I had twelve boys on the payroll then, back in the beginning, and they got from sixty to a hundred bucks a week. That took a big slice out of the fifteen hundred right away. Then there was the cops. Every flatfoot on the beat got a fin a week. The sergeants got ten. And Big Sam. took an envelope with a hundred in it every week to the captain at the precinct house to keep the other sons-of-bitches off our necks.

That wasn't the end of it. Every few months they'd switch the plain-clothes squad in our district and the new crew never had no trouble finding out where to come for the pay-off. You could knock a guy off under their nose and they couldn't see it, but they could smell a quick buck a mile away.

Even that wasn't enough. About once a month the federal revenue men would send word that they were having a plate of spaghetti at Luigi's or some other place and you had to get some more envelopes ready. Fifty bucks a week was the standard pay-off for them in those days. But at least they were honest back then. You bought them and they stayed bought. Not like now, when they are afraid to take a nickel because every federal agent has got two more on his tail to check up on him. Consequence is, today none of them have got a stake to fall back on does anything happen. All they got is a job, and the only way they can keep on holding it is by making a record. That means pinches all over the lot, and when an agent gets up on the stand he'll lie his god-damned head off just to hold his stinking job.

The way I see it, men like that can't have no respect for themselves.

But back in those early days they weren't any trouble. They took their pay and went their way, and did they have to make a pinch because of too many complaints, they let you know in advance so you could set things up. You hauled some bum in off the Bowery and shaved him up and put a clean shirt on him, and when the raid came he was the owner of the joint and took the rap.

That saved my own people from getting their records messed up down at Headquarters.

What with one thing and another, there were plenty of head-aches. After I had paid off my own outfit each week I had to hand in my contribution for the top men upstairs. Lucania handled that. I was lucky if I had a few hundred a week left in my pocket, and even that didn't last long.

There was always something. Some family in the block in trouble or the old man out of work or a kid getting in the kind of jam it takes money to fix. In the old days folks had gone to Mike Petrucci for help, but he wasn't around any more. In a way I felt responsible, so I didn't mind their coming to me instead. It made me feel good, and besides, I was building up for the future. It was all an investment, kind of.

But I wasn't making any hundred grand a year, like the newspapers said later.

In a way I got the cops to thank for what happened next. I never had any idea of getting mixed up in politics, but I was forced into it.

Seems like there wasn't no end to the kind of dirty stuff the cops would pull, did they get money-hungry. And all of a sudden they hit on a new swindle.

There were plenty of kids in our district that had had a bit at the reform school and young guys that had done a stretch up the river and were let out on parole. Being out on parole meant they couldn't stand a pinch of no kind. Did they get their name on a police blotter, they were sent back to finish their bit.

So some cheap bastard of a cop gets smart and has a brain wave and passes it on to a couple of other flatfeet. All they got to do is check up and find out which guys are out on parole and then lay in wait for them at night.

They'd get them on the way home from the poolroom or a game of cards or maybe just hanging around some corner chewing the fat with friends.

Out of nowhere comes a couple of cops.

"You, there! What do you think you're doing?"

"I ain't doing nothing."

"Don't get fresh, you dago punk. We've been watching you. You've been acting suspicious and loitering."

"You're crazy. I ain't loitering. I'm just walking home."

"Tell that to the captain down at the station house."

"Let go of me! I wasn't doing nothing, I tell you. I'm on parole. I'm keeping my nose clean."

"Come on. You want to get beat up for resisting an officer?"

But then on the way to the station house they'd get human. They'd brag about it.

"We're human, kid. We don't want to see you going back up the river for a stretch. And that's what will happen if we take you in and book you. Maybe this could be fixed."

"I ain't got no money of that kind."

"You know where to get some, don't you? Ain't you got any friends working for Little Tony?"

So in the middle of the night I'd get a ring or someone would come knocking at the door. Mostly it was chicken feed—thirty, forty bucks, or at most a half century. They was cheap bastards.

But it was a goddamned pain. The kind of petty grafting that ain't decent, picking on folks that can't help themselves. I'd get mad inside every time I had to shell out.

I bellyached to the district leader but that didn't do any good. He just spread his hands out and looked hopeless.

"I can't do anything about that, Tony. They're letting you run your stills and other stuff. Ain't that enough?"

"No."

But there wasn't any point in wasting words with him. He was a hang-over from the old days. He did what the mick machine downtown told him to do and got his pay in petty city contracts for his plastering company. To hell with what happened to the rest of the wops.

Then I got to figuring. There was all the families running stills for me, more than a hundred, and all their relatives. There were the boys that were in my outfit and all the ones that were looking to the day when they could belong. They had big families, too. On top of that were all the others you could swing into line with a word or two. It all added up to a lot of votes.

I made a meet with Lucania to talk things over. He listened carefully, then come up with a suggestion.

"You ought to get together with Lepke."

"Who's he?"

"He operates over in the Jew section. That's part of this ward. He's all right. We've done some business with him now and again."

That was how I first met Louis Buchalter. It didn't matter he wasn't a wop, we seemed to understand one another right away. At first I thought it was because he talked business, the way I did. Later I discovered we had other things in common.

He'd come up out of the streets the same as me, having to fight all the way. Having to use his head instead of his fists because, like me, he was small and thin. He was quiet and soft-spoken, even when he got double-crossed and had to order somebody knocked off, and in all the years I was dealing with him his word was better than money in the bank.

That first meeting it turned out that Louis had been running into the same trouble I had. Every cop and his brother putting the bite on and protection costing too much money. I came up with my idea.

"We ought to get our own men in. Pick our own district leader and later plant a couple of men on the magistrates' bench where they will do us some good."

"A Jew don't stand a chance in this ward. Come election time, the micks and you wops start yelling Christ-killer."

"That ain't nothing to what the micks call us. So what? Between your people and mine we could swing enough votes to bury the goddamned Irishers did we want to."

We talked it back and forth, getting it. worked out what we should do. The outcome was I should go ahead and do what I could. Louis promised to swing all the weight he could in his neighborhood when it came to a showdown.

It wasn't any secret who the real political boss was in those days. He was a big, husky mick living way up in the Bronx. He hadn't never done anything but politics since he was out of knee pants. Did anyone need a quick fix for a city building permit or to keep a rat-trap slum from being torn down or to buy a job as a cop, the word was always "See Jimmy H."

So I pulled some strings to get to see him. I learned early that there was never no point in wasting time with anybody but the main guy.

He had a smooth, easy way that could fool you if you didn't watch careful.

"Well, my boy, and what can I do for you?"

"Nothing. I figure it's the other way around."

He stopped whatever he had started to say and gave me a hard look. "What's that again, my boy?"

I laid it straight on the line.

"You're going to lose a lot of votes in my neighborhood, come next election. A lot of us ain't satisfied with the breaks we been getting."

He shook his head, as though what I was saying didn't make sense.

"You must be mistaken. You've got one of your own as district leader, a fine upstanding Eyetalian gentleman with the best interests of his people at heart. You sound as though you'd been listening to some dirty Protestant Republicans, my boy."

"I ain't been listening to nobody. I'm just fed up with my people having no protection from a bunch of cheap, grafting bastards in uniform. From now on we want something in return for our votes."

"Perhaps after the next election ..."

I didn't give him time to finish. I picked up my hat and walked out. I'd given him the score. Now he had to find out for himself it wasn't just empty words.

The city primaries were a little over three months away and already it was in the bag what would happen. Like always before, they'd picked a mick and a Jew to run against each other all the way down the slate, figuring that in the end the wops would throw in with the micks because they was both Catholics. They put a few Italian names in here and there to make it look good, but they didn't count for nothing.

I got together with Lepke again. Seems the brother of one of the boys in his outfit was a lawyer. He was some kind of crazy radical, but he was a bug on politics and knew his way around blindfolded. What to do about filing for office, and write-ins, and getting up lists of signatures, and stuff like that.

We gave him a grand for expense money and a list of names. I'd picked a cousin of Big Sam's to run for councilman. He was two or three years out of law school and I'd thrown a few cases his way when some of my boys got picked up for one thing or another. The way he'd fight in court you'd think he was trying to save them from the hot seat instead of maybe six months on the Island. He was too hotheaded to have been any good in the rackets, but he gave you your money's worth as a mouthpiece.

In the beginning none of the regular party men paid much attention to what we were doing. We didn't make no big fuss, we only stuck up a few cards and posters here and there to make it look amateur and legitimate.

The important work we had to do was on the quiet.

I went personal to all the families that were running stills for me and laid down the law.

"You want to keep on making alky for me?"

"Sure thing I do. Whatsa mat'? I do something wrong?"

"Not yet. Only you will if you don't vote the way I say come elections."

"But Vittorio—"

"Who's paying you, him or me? You send Vittorio to me when he comes around."

So the next thing I know, the district leader is hunting me up.

"What you trying to do to me, Tony?"

"Who said I'm doing anything?"

"When I see my people they tell me they got to vote the way you say."

"So what are you worrying about? They never vote but one way, do they?"

Come primary day we knew what to do in the polling places where we wouldn't run up any votes. Both Lepke and I had learned that young, when we were still in short pants hungry for a handful of change. We passed the word down to our boys and they rounded up a bunch of kid gangs and set them to raising hell in the Irish section, heaving stones and stink bombs through the windows of the polling places. A lot of biddies who would have voted for the first time changed their minds and went home.

I had my own outfit in order. I had forty guys out personally taking every wop family down to vote and putting the fear of God into them did anybody but Joe Santoro get on the ballot for councilman and the rest of our slate the same way.

Over in his section Lepke was following through on his end. I heard later that one of his boys named Bugsy Siegel, who was nothing but a kid killer at the time, went to routing whole families out at gunpoint and marching them down to the polls.

Between the riots in the mick section and our own voters we did all right. As far as the local stuff went, we knocked hell out of the machine slate. It maybe wouldn't mean so much by itself, but it was a way of showing power.

Early the next morning the district leader was pounding on my door. When he started talking he screamed so loud you couldn't make out whether he was crying or blowing his top.

"You trying to ruin me? You make a fool out of me! For twenty years I've been a good party man, running things without any trouble, and then out of nowhere you come and wreck it all. What am I going to tell the boss—that I don't know my own people any more?"

"You ain't going to tell him anything."

"I got to. Already he sent word I should come uptown to explain."

"I'll do the explaining. You go home." All of a sudden I felt sorry for him standing there with a dumb look on his face, still not understanding what had happened. I said, "Go home and take it easy, Vittorio. You got no worries. I'll see that you're taken care of."

He had enough guts to curse at me. in Italian but I didn't bother to answer.

It wasn't his fault he hadn't changed with the times.

This time when I got in to see Jimmy H. he didn't have the same easy manner he had had before, like he was just listening to be polite. There were red splotches on his face, and his eyes when he stared at me were a cold, fishy blue.

"I understand you're behind this damned nonsense that made a monkey out of Vittorio."

I shrugged. "I told you there was trouble down in my district. You didn't want to listen."

"We've handled troublemakers before. Young lads who got too big for their britches. I hear you're running a string of stills in your neighborhood. Tomorrow the police will start doing their duty."

"If they do they'll starve to death!" In those days I always got mad inside when somebody started making threats, but now I tried to keep from flaring up. "I'm paying in over a grand a month to the cops and the higher-ups at the precinct house. They ain't going to to like it none if you take it away from them. I don't mind paying it—it's a legitimate business expense."

"What in hell are you raising a fuss for, then?"

"Because I'm tired of us wops being pushed around by a bunch of ignorant bastards in uniform that think every day is Christmas. Cops putting the squeeze on kids just out of reform school that ain't done nothing so that they can get an extra saw-buck to take some cheap floozie out with. From now on we want a voice in things."

"You could talk it over with Vittorio—"

"To hell with Vittorio. He's still an old-country guinea think-ing he's in heaven because he's got a white shirt and a business and folks to call him mister. We want our own leader—someone we pick ourselves." I figured it was time to bring matters to a head, so I got up like I was ready to leave. "You should remember this: There's more wops in New York now than there is in Rome. And they're beginning to wake up. They ain't going to take no more pushing around. What happened yesterday down in our ward was just a sample."

He didn't say anything. I turned and started out, but when I reached the door he spoke up.

"Come back and sit down, my boy. We haven't finished talk-ing yet."

It wasn't all one way. I'd heard stories. I knew the different mobs that were springing up around town were kicking in to him. I brought up the subject myself, saying I was willing to send a little contribution uptown every month for party expenses. Five C notes a month to start with, and more if things worked out O.K. We'd get our own district leader and the regular party would get behind Joe Santoro and see that he got places. And the next time there was an opening on the magistrates' bench we'd get a break there.

So now I'm in politics.

Fifteen and twenty years later I was to read a lot of stories about how the underworld had corrupted politics and bought up the police and courts and the law in this place and that. You don't buy anything that ain't for sale.

All we was ever trying to do was get a break and protect our own. It was just a matter of business.

A couple of other important things happened at the same time. The last of the fighting as to who should head up the Maffia downtown and over in Brooklyn had ended, with Joe "The Boss" Masseria moving into power.

That meant that Lucania was sitting pretty. And it looked like I had played my cards right stringing along with him all the way. He was my contact with the top men in the Unione Siciliano, which was what they were calling the Maffia now, and it seemed like I couldn't have no one better.

Then something happened overnight to almost change the picture.

Lucania was picked up out of a ditch one morning early over in Staten Island. First off they thought he was dead, he was so badly beat up and cut. But he was still breathing when the police ambulance got there, and one way or another the croakers pulled him through. But the way they left his face his own mother wouldn't have recognized him.

When the word got out everyone figured there was another war on inside the family and that maybe Masseria would be next. The only thing that didn't make good sense was the way Lucania had been taken for a ride. It didn't look professional, the way he'd just been beat up and left living. It was amateur stuff.

I had to wait nearly three weeks before I got a chance to see him personal. During that time I didn't turn over his weekly cut on my business to nobody. A couple of guys came around to see me, telling me that they were collecting in his place, but I didn't give them the time of day.

"I don't know what you're talking about. What deals Lucania and I got are private."

I liked to see clear what was ahead before I took my quick jump.

Then finally I got around to seeing Lucania. He was out of the hospital but still couldn't hit the street. His face was all done up in bandages and you could see easy it hurt him when he moved.

"Who did it, Salvatore? Anybody I can take care of?"

"No. Not unless you want Mr. Whiskers on your tail."

"I don't get it."

He gave me the story then. It was the kind that couldn't ever come out in public for a lot of reasons. Seems like he and some of the top men in the Unione had a stack of money invested in a shipment of narcotics coming in on a freighter from Greece. The trouble was, the word had got out in the wrong places, and Lucania was over scouting the docks on the Island, making sure there wouldn't be any double cross at the last moment.

A couple of narcotic agents who had got a tip that something was in the wind were over at the same time, trying to get a lead on what parties to put the bite on. They spotted Lucania and put two and two together and grabbed him.

When he wouldn't give with the information they wanted they started working on him.

"They didn't like it I was calling them their right names. They was crooked sons-of-bitches it don't do no good to pay off. They'd wind up making a pinch anyway."

"Couldn't we frame them?"

"Later, maybe."

Like I said, some people had made the mistake of reading the signs wrong, figuring right off that it was thumbs down on Lucania on account of some family fight among the Unione big shots. He had a couple of words to say about them.

"In a way I'm glad it happened. It showed me who I could trust. And that's going to be important from now on."

He tipped me off to something else then. He was due to move in as right-hand man of Joe "The Boss" Masseria. From the way he talked I got the idea that in time he might be a little more than that.

"The boss is all right. He swings a lot of weight with the old-timers that are still important in the Unione. But times have changed, Tony. You know it and I know it. It takes young guys to run things now."

I said carefully, "You can always count on me, Salvatore."

He let me know something else then. He wasn't calling himself Salvatore any more. That was old-country stuff and from now on everything was going to be American and up-to-date. And he was even changing the way he spelled his last name.

The boys had already give him a nickname because of the way he pulled through when everybody thought he was the next thing to dead. Lucky, they called him.

That was how he was known after that.

Charles "Lucky" Luciano.

CHAPTER SEVEN

I T WAS hard to be businesslike in those days. There was too much easy money around and too many different gangs fighting for it. And when they wasn't gunning for one another they was looking for fancy ways of letting everyone know how much dough they had.

It wasn't enough any more to be a big shot in the neighborhood. Now you had to own a piece of Broadway at the same time to be rated as somebody important.

It was supposed to be business to cut yourself in on a night club or a musical comedy, but it was only an excuse for dames and making a big splurge. What happened was some of the boys took a shine to some Broadway stars and then discovered they couldn't buy them for cash on the line, no matter did they offer them a thousand bucks for a night. But it was different when they came up with the idea of headlining them in a fancy night club or a musical show. Then it was all between friends, and being a push-over didn't count.

I didn't want any part of it but I couldn't keep some of my boys from having ideas. Big Sam in particular. He was always coming up with reminders of what some of the other mobs were doing. Were they Jews or micks I could brush it off, but when some of our own people started doing the same I didn't have any ready answer.

Big Sam would always work around to the subject easy.

"You know the Gap from up in East Harlem?"

"Uh-huh."

"He just bought himself a piece of the Casino, that fancy French joint that's opening up next week."

"O.K. So we'll make a visit and drop him a bundle."

That was a custom then. It still is, for that matter. Does a wop who is a right guy open up a bar or a restaurant or a club of some kind, the head men of the neighborhood mobs pay him a visit opening night. You take a party with you, the bigger the better, and set drinks up all around. Whatever the check comes to you drop a couple of extra century notes alongside. It gives the new business a break and lets the guy know who his friends are.

It's a nice friendly idea.

Big Sam wasn't willing to let it go at that. He had other things in mind.

"The Gap ain't no more important than you are. We could have a piece of any of two or three better joints, did you say the word."

"I got plenty of headaches now."

"It wouldn't mean no work for you. I could handle everything easy."

"Handle the dames, you mean."

That was the way it went. The underworld wasn't no different from anyplace else. You had to keep up the same kind of front as your competitors or the word would get around that you weren't doing so well. You could have a million dollars in the bank, but unless some of it showed it didn't count.

But there was another angle to the Broadway business that Sam didn't think to mention. Having a night club or a show with chorus girls in your pocket was a break when it came to keeping the politicians and judges and the like happy. Offer to take them to a two-buck whore house and they'd spit in your face, but give the same stuffed shirts a chance to get in some dressing rooms backstage where they could cop a couple of free looks and a date for afterward and they got to believing they were big-time play-boys all on their own.

One way or another you were buying them with some flesh that was for sale, except that over on Broadway the setup went by another name. But politicians never have any trouble kidding themselves they are getting by on their own.

So every time Big Sam kept bringing up the subject, with me brushing it aside, I knew that sooner or later I would have to play along with the rest. I could tell by the way some of my boys were looking at me that they didn't like not having a finger in show business like the other mobs. In the twenties you had to have a couple of blonde chorus babes to parade about to advertise you was up on top, just like later on it had to be black Cadillacs. Always some damned thing.

I was beefing about it one night to Lepke when we got together to discuss a little business deal. He was running into the same kind of trouble.

Siegel, the same Bugsy who had herded the voters down to the polls at gunpoint, was giving him a headache.

"He's a good boy, but too temperamental. That's the trouble with this business, Tony. We have to handle too many prima donnas."

That was the way he talked. Smooth and easy, not calling them a bunch of goddamned tail chasers, the way I felt like doing.

I said as much.

"If they were any different, Tony, they wouldn't be working for us. They'd be smart enough to figure percentages and have some business of their own. When you come right down to it, a hoodlum is nothing but a gutter brat who never grew up."

I got to thinking then of the things I had wanted when I was a kid scrambling for pennies and what I could pick up. Fancy clothes and flashy cars and a diamond as big as a marble on the little finger of my left hand where it would show off best. Later stuff like that hadn't seemed important. Most of the time I'd been too busy keeping things in order and planning for the future. Playing big for the neighborhood bums was something that didn't pay off.

All I wanted now was a decent place to live, and it seemed like there I was caught in a trap. I had the money—I could have had myself one of those fancy places up on Seventh Avenue without even feeling the bite. Only everything I had was tied up in the district and the slums where I was born. That was where the boys on my payroll lived, and the families that worked my stills, and the Italian lottery customers, and all the other little odds and ends of business I had. That was where I was backing Joe Santoro to go places in the political machine and seeing that Tramaglino, the new district leader, didn't start getting himself a swelled head.

I had to be on hand all the time, twenty-four hours a day, did something go wrong. And there was always something to settle.

Always something …

I'd fixed me up a place to live as best I could. I'd taken the whole floor_ up over Chico's barbershop and fixed it up almost the way I wanted it. That meant going personal over to one of the big furniture stores on Fifth Avenue and laying it on the line. I got hold of one of the main guys and tried to describe the kind of stuff I'd seen in those fancy apartments on Seventh Avenue.

"Was it Empire? Louis the Fifteenth, perhaps?"

"I wouldn't know. You show it to me and I can say yes or no."

The goddamned window curtains cost more than two hundred bucks each and the rug in the front room could have paid the rent for a year. The same with everything else. I figured maybe I was in the wrong racket if all you had to do was take some spindly sticks of wood and slap some gold leaf on and charge like it was the mayor's chair that was for sale. Maybe the guy selling the stuff thought I was nuts, too, because he looked kind of funny when I had to take him and a couple of his workmen over to the flat to make measurements.

"You're certain, sir, that you aren't making a mistake in the type of furnishings you have selected?"

"I know what I want."

"I only meant it is quite a bit of money to spend."

"I'm paying cash."

I knew what he meant. It was the kind of layout that didn't belong on the edge of the slums. But what were you going to do when you can't get out yourself?

I fixed up a kind of office on the ground floor back of the barbershop and didn't allow nobody but Big Sam upstairs. I didn't want no bums cluttering up the place and spilling ashes all over everywhere and maybe spitting in the corners. More, I wanted it to be private, so that when I pulled the curtains I could be a million miles from the stinking street outside.

It knocked Big Sam over the first time he seen it complete.

"Jeez, Tony! It's like something out of a picture book. I'll be afraid to sit down heavy anywhere."

"You'd better be."

"And a piano, yet. What the hell you want with that? Ain't nobody we know can play one."

"What you want with three dames on the string? You can't go out with only one at a time."

"I like knowing I've got them."

"O.K. I like knowing I've got a piano, do I sometime meet up with a party can handle one. And I don't mean none of this goddamned ragtime junk."

I knew the kind of music I liked—the kind I'd heard snatches of all my life. When I was a kid delivering stuff for Black Tony over on the West Side I used to stand in front of the Opera House or Carnegie Hall and read the posters and wonder did I have the guts to buy a ticket in, Was it night maybe there would be cars with chauffeurs driving up and dames painted up worse than any of the two-bit whores at Dirty Mamie's stepping out. They would be weighed down with a million dollars' worth of rocks and the cops would get busy pushing everybody out of the way like they were dirt.

It was wop music and wop singers, but if you was a wop kid stopping on the street you couldn't even look.

It would be different someday, I'd tell myself.

Now I had myself one of those big Victrolas. I got a lot of Verdi and Puccini and Donizetti records, and when night came I could sit there listening and smoking a good cigar and forgetting for a while things were the way they were on the outside.

But it never lasted long.

Like in any other business, you had to keep moving. You couldn't never rest and take things easy. If you stood still some other mob would catch up with you and pass you by. It wasn't enough now just to turn out straight alky and sell it in cans. You had to have your own doctoring plant and pour the stuff into bottles and slap phony labels on. You had to get hold of real stuff to spread around among the politicians and so the guys in the cutting end would know what the hell real whisky or Scotch tasted like. You had to make arrangements with the Dutchman or Waxy Gordon's oufit for beer for the speaks in your district and keep on their tail to see they didn't hand you nothing but needled slop.

A million headaches all the time.

What made it worse was all the gang fights going on. Punks knocking one another off all over the place. Every time that happened there would be a lot of crap written up in the newspapers, and if you didn't know better you'd think that hoodlums with machine guns had taken over the city.

It gave the whole business a bad name.

Things weren't going so well inside the Unione at the same time. The old-country men like Masseria that headed it up didn't have any imagination. They didn't realize that things had changed and it wasn't enough any more to have a society that was just feeding off itself. You had to start thinking big and planning big.

That didn't mean like Capone was doing over in Chicago. Johnny Torrio had started him on his way there, taking him over from Brooklyn when Big Jim Colosimo out there came east for a couple of gunmen to help him out in some trouble. From then on Capone started taking over.

He wasn't strictly speaking an inside member of the Unione, not being from Sicily, but he got Unione help all along the line. And he was doing all right, except he began thinking and acting like he was God Almighty.

But he was the kind of man they needed for those days in a place like Chicago. Luciano called the turn once when he said, "That's a crazy goddamned town! They ain't got no respect for law or nothing out there. A man's life ain't safe out on the streets."

Even so, him acting like he did out there didn't make things easy in New York. A lot of young punks thought all they had to do was take a gun and go kill somebody to be a second Capone. You had to keep batting their ears down to keep them in line, and sometimes you had to wipe them off the slate entirely.

When their bodies were picked up in some alley afterward it was always written up as a gang killing. But it wasn't. It was just a way of protecting everybody from a few lugs that were trigger-happy.

Somebody has to keep things in order.

That was one of the troubles with Joe "The Boss" Masseria. His only idea of how to settle trouble was to send someone out with a knife or a gun, like in the old days. Lucky had different ideas—he was smarter when it came to using his head. He was the one who first wanted to make it so the Unione would tie in on working agreements with a few top outsiders instead of just sticking to our own people.

"With a bunch of muscle boys you can only control just so much territory," he used to say to me. "Even then some outfit with more guns can come along and clean you out. But if you got enough money and use it right you could control the whole goddamned country. There wouldn't be nothing could stop you."

It was a dream, kind of, he had. I could understand easy what was in his mind. Did the day ever come when we had that kind of power, we wouldn't be operating just in the slums no more.

We could live where we wanted to, as we wanted to. We could go tell all the cops in the world to go kiss us in the same place they'd booted us as kids and make them like it. Like it so much they'd come back for more.

I said the way I said all along through the years, "You can count on me when the time comes, Salvatore."

"Lucky. Call me Lucky."

"O.K., Lucky."

It wasn't long before I understood why he was superstitious about his new name. He needed luck for what was coming up. It happened one afternoon in a bar over in Sheepshead Bay. Joe Masseria had a meeting there and Luciano was with him as always. Comes a time when Luciano looks at his watch and decides he has to go to the water closet.

He wasn't gone more than three, four minutes, but that was enough. He could hear the shots from the men's room.

When he got back into the bar Masseria was sprawled out on the floor, bleeding from his stomach and a hole in his head. Nobody knew who done it except that it was three strangers with guns. It didn't matter.

What counted was that from now on Lucky was the boss.

Like he said, times had changed and it took young guys with modern ideas to run things.

CHAPTER EIGHT

W E HAD a meeting a little while after that, Lucky and Lepke and me. We had a deal in liquor cooking, financing a shipload of legitimate stuff. It was Lepke who had made the contact. None of the New York mobs went in for real rum-running in those days. That was all handled by an outfit with headquarters up in Massachusetts that owned a flock of boats that brought the stuff down from St. Pierre and Miquelon, a couple of islands way the hell and gone the other side of Newfoundland. The ships anchored ten, twenty miles off Long Island or New Jersey or some other place, and from then on landing the stuff was your own headache.

Lucky was all for coming up with the money needed himself, but I had a different idea. Santoro had been picking up information down at City Hall and passing it back to me and after that I had done some investigating on my own through some of the contacts Big Sam had made over on Broadway.

"We don't need to use our own money. We can borrow it."

Lucky looked at me like I was talking simple. "What kind of Shylocks are going to lend you fifty, sixty grand?"

"A bank."

"You know better than that, Tony. We ain't going in for no stick-ups these days."

"I ain't talking about no stick-ups. I'm talking about this Jew named Rothstein over to the West Side. He goes down to the bank with you and writes his name on the back of your note and you get the dough you want. He gets cut in for thirty per cent of the take, when and if."

"Why pay some bastard for money we don't need?"

"Because we get more than just money when we deal with him."

I went on giving the low-down on the things I had learned. Arnold Rothstein had been on the scene a long time, way back before the Prohibition mobs started. Up to now everbody had thought of him as just a big-time gambler and a smart percentage guy. It hadn't been no secret that he had paid off the fix for the Chicago White Sox to throw the World Series a few years back. Things like that he was an expert at.

But I'd found out he was even smarter at other things. He was the man the crooks and thieves dealt with, both before and after they pulled a job. Did they need money to case a joint or to set up a sucker in a confidence game, they went to him. And did somthing go wrong, so the law nabbed them, they went to him again. He was a fixer, with a finger in every political puddle in town. He even kept his own outfit of shysters downtown, who could make a jury believe black was white when they started talking in a courtroom. The consequence was, Rothstein made more money than all the crooks in town put together. What it came down to was that most of them were working for him without ever waking up to the fact.

He was the kind of man I wanted to do business with. I figured I could learn something, did I keep my eyes open and my mouth shut. I wanted to find out what went on with big banks that would have thrown me out had I gone in alone to proposition them but could be eased into financing deals that were strictly the other side of the law if the right party said yes.

I wanted to find out some other things, mainly what made a guy like Rothstein so powerful. He didn't have no mob or no hired gunmen. Just money and connections. And the brains to know how to use them.

"We're all right when it comes to operating neighborhood mobs," I reminded Lucky. "But when we get outside our own territory we don't know from nothing. Like you said before, times have changed. We got to learn how real businessmen handle things."

So finally Lucky gave the word and that was the beginning of that.

It was a funny thing, but Lepke never got on too well with Rothstein. You would have thought the two being Jews they would wind up real friends, but Lepke wasn't having any.

"I don't trust him, Tony. At heart he's a goniff. Sooner or later he'll outsmart himself."

"Right now he knows all the ropes."

"He'll wind up hanging himself with one."

But that didn't stop our doing business with him. We made three loans from him that first year, a couple of times on rum-running deals and once when I needed an extra ten grand to pick up a batch of pin-ball machines to spread out through the district. I discovered quick enough how it was he worked things at the banks. Seems like he owned two or three apartment houses and a small hotel outright. He had them set up in corporations that added up to a credit of four or five hundred grand in the places where they figure such things out. That was all that counted when he walked into one of the banks he had dealings with.

You signed with the bank for the money and he backed the loan up with his name. What it amounted to was that he was making his cut without putting up no actual dough of his own at all.

It was smart.

The more I thought about it, the more I could see different angles. Up to then did any of us have extra cash we stashed it away in a strongbox somewhere handy so we could grab it quick did the need come up. I saw now how you could make the same dough work two ways. And I could see something else. Did you own buildings and property and such-like, you were legitimate all the way around, no matter where the money came from in the first place. You couldn't get fingered by the cops or the newspapers as just a mobster. You were a legitimate businessman.

That meant you could get by doors that had been closed to you before. You could talk to the kind of high-powered lawyers and connections that wouldn't give the time of day to underworld money but would grab the same dough if it had a different label on it. Just like the banks that wouldn't give me two bucks to open a peanut stand on my own say-so but would lay out fifty grand for a rum-running deal on the word of a crook like Rothstein.

Learning such things and seeing how they worked was a break for me. Up to then I'd just thought of money as so much cash with which you bought what you needed. Now I saw that it was a power in itself, more powerful in lots of ways than any mob that could ever be got together.

I talked it over with Lucky.

"This gold mine we got now ain't going to last forever. There's a lot of people got their bellyful of Prohibition. Come another election or two and they'll wipe it off the slate. Then what?"

"We'll find something else to make a buck on."

"We ought to be finding it now. And we don't have to look far if we're smart."

I'd spent a lot of time figuring just one angle out. That was pin-ball and slot machines. I'd looked into it and found there were just two factories in the country that turned them out. And they must have had some kind of agreement, because the price was about the same.

The angle was that in most places the machines were against the law, did anyone bother to look the law up. Usually the cops were the only ones who did, so they could collect a little more easy graft. On top of that, the machines were mostly owned and controlled by underworld outfits. Broken up in small lots like that, the take wasn't much, but it helped meet the weekly payrolls.

The thing that hit me was that here was a couple of strictly legitimate outfits not breaking no law or nothing but making a wad of dough dealing only with outfits like mine. And it was guys like me that had to pay the graft and have the headaches and take the rap for being underworld bosses whenever there was a clean-up campaign on and they threw a couple of the slot machines out on the street so the newspapers could take pictures of some police commissioner with a white flower stuck in his buttonhole smashing them up with a fire ax.

Likely me or some other guy like me had paid for the flower on top of everything.

The way I looked at it, we ought to own one of those factories, or at least as big a piece of one as we could grab.

"Suppose they throw us out on our can, do we walk in with a proposition like that?" Lucky wanted to know.

"Then they can start throwing their machines in the same place. The Unione swings enough weight here and around the country to make things tough. Lepke's got good contacts with the Bernstein outfit over in Detroit. They'll play ball with us. So will a lot of other mobs throughout the country in return for favors we might be able to do later. The factory either does business our way or it don't do no business at all."

It took time to work out the details. We picked the factory with which the mobs did the most business and then Lepke got hold of some tax experts he knew to get a line on what the outfit was worth. Then I had Rothstein arrange a meet for me with a couple of men with offices down in Wall Street. I figured they were strictly wrong ones if they were tied up with him, but for what was wanted they could do without asking too many questions. That was to make an offer for 50 per cent of the works at the market value.

They got turned down quick but we'd already figured on that.

The next three or four months the factory out in Illinois must have wondered what hit them. First they began to get a flock of cancellations. Then they began having labor trouble. Lucky happened to remember that one of the Capone outfit, a mick named Murray "The Camel" Humphries, was an expert on stuff like that. Then to wind things up there was more trouble with their delivery trucks and plant machinery that came from hand-fuls of emery dust dumped here and there. But none of it was the kind of trouble they could blame on a Wall Street office that had made a legitimate business offer in a legitimate business way.

So the second time we made an offer it wasn't turned down so quick, and the third time they grabbed it, likely figuring they were taking us for suckers.

But after that there wasn't no labor trouble or any other kind. We had plenty of customers and we were able to jack up the prices twenty-five to fifty bucks a model without any kicks. It was the kind of business I liked, where you had your fingers at both ends and in the middle and could see what was happening all down the line.

Lepke had been doing some spreading out on his own and he cut me in on a couple of deals. At first it was just strike-breaking stuff, but soon he began to get other ideas and see how there was a way of making money from both sides. Since those days I've read a lot of crap about how the underworld moved in on unions and labor rackets and I get disgusted every time I do. Like always, it's guys like me and Lepke and Lucky that get the rap. You'd think we invented the whole dirty business.

Truth is, it was the bosses, the respectable owners who would yell copper if you looked at them cross-eyed, who first started doing business with what the papers call the underworld. But it wasn't even the underworld—it was just rock-headed hoodlums off the streets. That happened every time some bunch of workers tried to form a union or if they got one together and finally got enough guts to pull a strike. Then the owners would send out the word for a gang of hoodlums to bust things up. Only they didn't call them that. They was plant guards or some other high-sounding name and they had police protection while they was busting heads.

Lepke didn't like it none. He had the same ideas as me back in the days when I was talking things over with Red Nolan out at the Farms.

"We're getting played for suckers, doing somebody else's dirty work. It's our own people mostly in those sweatshops, Tony. Jews and dagos like ourselves."

I agreed with him. But I still couldn't see any answer. Then it came when we weren't looking for it.

What happened was that a bunch of movie houses figured a way they could squeeze out a few extra bucks a week profit. At the time there was only one union for movie operators. It was a nice tight little setup. It cost five hundred to join, but once you were in you pretty near always had a job. The union insisted on two operators being in the booth at all times, and pay started at sixty-five bucks a week, which was good wages for a square john in those days.

So the smaller movie houses decided they didn't need but one operator in the booth at a time and that sixty-five bucks was too much money anyway.

That was when they came to Lepke. The idea was he should start a new union with different rules. One man in a booth at a time and less dough per week. They had the cash to lay on the line to start things off and the promise of more if things worked out right.

First off Lepke was of two minds what to do, but then he got to thinking things out. That was when he saw the angle that was to turn into a gold mine for us later on.

"They're stupid, Tony. They can't see beyond making an extra dollar by cutting down expenses. What happens if we start a new union and it takes over?"

"That's easy. We take over."

I could see the pattern then, the one I'd always been looking for. By themselves most of the small unions didn't have any power. They tried doing things legitimate and got locked out and beat up for their pains. But if men who knew how to fight back moved in and took over, then it would be different. Men like me and Lepke who had learned how to organize the hard way back when we were kids working in the protection rackets or heaving stink bombs to bust up election meetings. We knew how to handle the cops, too, did they get ideas.

There wasn't no need to stop with a movie operators' union. If it worked there, it could work other places—in the garment section and the building trades and on the docks and every other place you could think of.

It was a natural all the way around. Ready and waiting because some sons-of-bitches were too greedy to look ahead. And it was all legitimate.

Yet all the while we were looking around for new angles and new opportunities, there were the old lines to keep going. Bootlegging was getting to be more of a headache every day, with the cops and revenue agents getting hungrier for graft and cheap competition cutting in everywhere.

I'd bought a piece of a night club over on the West Side off Broadway and let Big Sam front for it. It was what he liked—he was happy could he sit at a big table surrounded by flashy dames and set up drinks for the house. Pretty soon he began keeping one of them steady—a big tall babe that did an act at the club. He wanted me to come look at her to show how things had changed since the early days of Angie or one of the other neighborhood brats on the roof.

"She's a real star, Tony. She gets her name and picture in the papers all the time. There ain't nothing cheap about her. The real stuff."

So to please him I go take a look at her. She can't sing no more than I can and she dances about the same way. What she does is come out in the spotlight in a lot of flowing stuff of some kind and she has a couple of trained parrots that keep pecking away and unpinning things until she winds up naked as when she was born. Better looking, maybe, but just as bare.

"She's O.K., ain't she, Tony? She's all right."

"I don't see nothing missing. She's got it all out for everyone to see."

"But that's business. She's an artist, like. She don't put out for nobody but me, though."

"I seen another act last week in the Gap's place. A hot-looking dame who makes love to a snake right in front of everybody. Maybe I could arrange a meet for you."

"Aw, Tony. I wouldn't want no babe that was two-timing me in public like that. You ought to know me better."

Night clubs were funny places in those days. They ain't never made no good sense to me, but then they made less so. Nobody but mobsters and rich folks could afford to hang out in them, the way the prices were rigged. So the result was you had society people from Park Avenue rubbing up against hoodlums and glad to make the acquaintance. The women were painted up like whores, and with a couple of drinks in them they acted worse, and you wondered their men didn't have enough respect for themselves to slap them into line. That's something I ain't never been able to understand about people that are supposed to be strictly legitimate. They ain't got any morals, or if they've got them they don't show. In the slums a woman is strictly one thing or another—she's either respectable or she's a whore, no matter what kind of story she tries to put up. There ain't no halfway business and she gets treated according to what she is.

But once you get outside the slums you don't know what the hell the score is. Some of the boys got into bad trouble from figuring some society dame was easy because she acted that way and then having her yell for the law when they tried to push her over.

That was one thing I made Big Sam be tough about at the club.

"See to it that our boys lay off the society dames like they was poison. I don't want no rumbles with the law over nothing."

"Suppose they fall for one of 'em? What can I do?"

"If it's one of our boys, fix things up with one of your chorus girls. He'll get over it quick enough. And if it's some bitch from Park Avenue, slip her a micky."

You had to draw the line somewhere."

CHAPTER NINE

WAS having my own troubles as far as women went. One woman, that is. It had started a long time back, without my ever intending anything like that should happen. I had too many other things on my mind, and dames were a dime a dozen.

It began routine, with a neighborhood kid named Vito that was always getting in one jam after another. Stupid stuff that didn't make no sense, just throwing his weight around because he had to be a wise guy. You couldn't talk sense to him—he knew more than everybody else.

So every five, six months his sister had to come to me because the cops somewhere had grabbed him. I couldn't keep him from doing an early stretch out at the Protectorate, and what meanness he wasn't born with he finished learning there. Mostly, though, I managed to square things one way or another.

I could see it made her ashamed.

"I wouldn't bother you all the time, Tony, if it weren't for Mamma. She believes everything Vito tells her, and according to him he never did anything wrong."

"Forget it."

"There isn't any way we can ever pay you back."

"I said forget it."

I liked seeing her and talking to her. Teresa was maybe seventeen, eighteen back then. She was working behind the counter at a five-and-ten across town and still going to night school. Always she dressed neat and smart, without throwing herself around like most of the other girls. She was good-looking with kind of creamy white skin and soft clear brown eyes, but you had to look twice to notice it.

There was just her and Vito and the old lady in the family, and I didn't need nobody to tell me that it was the few bucks she earned that paid the rent and brought in the food.

So the windup is I put Vito on the payroll. He was a punk you couldn't trust, but I told Big Sam to keep him doing simple things like servicing the pin-ball machines or picking up alky empties.

Even so it didn't do no good. His dough was gone before he got it in an alley crap game or playing big shot to a couple of cheap floozies. And he was always stepping out of line, always trying to pull a fast one of some kind.

Teresa knew what the score was. I tried sending around a few bucks a week to her old lady, giving her some story it was dough held out of Vito's pay, but Teresa wasn't having any.

"You've done enough for us, Tony. We're not taking charity while I can still work."

"I told you it was dough due Vito. Only he don't know it."

"You're lying."

"O.K., I'm lying. But why should you have to pay the freight for everything?"

"Why should you?"

I didn't have any answer to that one. I didn't know myself. Or maybe it was that I didn't want to know. I told myself I was just playing it the way I'd want someone else to play it was Teresa my sister.

It wasn't any good figuring anything else. I'd worked that out long ago in my mind, watching other guys in my fix that got themselves tied up steady to some woman and wound up married. It never worked out good. Women don't like having a man they can't count on to be with them so many hours a day. And if you are in the rackets you never know where you are going to be or when. So they sit home waiting for you, worrying even though you tell them not to, and you show when you can. Sometimes it's just a couple of hours you are late and sometimes a couple of days does something break wrong somewhere.

It ain't any good. You start yelling at one another and if you've got any real feeling it makes you weak at the wrong time. Guys that were happy married and then got nabbed for something and did a stretch in the can told me how tough it was.

"When I was single I could do a bit standing on my ear, Tony. But it's different when you're just married. Then you're serving two sentences. One behind the goddamned bars and the other in your mind, thinking about things at home."

After that their judgment wasn't never hard and quick like it ought to be. They tried to play it safe, and there ain't no way of playing it safe in our business.

So I didn't get any ideas. Teresa was a decent girl who was getting a lousy break and that was all. Could I help a little, it didn't cost nothing and didn't do no harm. Like I would do something for one of the family.

One time I got to talking to her about what she had in mind to do. That was the month she finished high school in night classes.

"Now that you're all educated, what comes next? Should I start saving up for a wedding present?"

She didn't answer right away. When she did she started by shaking her head.

"No. That goes for both your questions. There isn't any boy I'll be marrying this year or next. And I'm not even half educated yet."

"You ain't telling me you want to be no schoolteacher?"

She smiled a little. "No again. You promise not to think I'm crazy if I tell you, Tony?"

"I won't think you're crazy."

"Well, then, if things were different I'd like to be a doctor. I'd settle for being a nurse, even, but what I'd really like is to be an honest-to-goodness doctor. That's what I've wanted ever since I was a little girl playing dolls. But what's the use of dreaming?"

I could have given her one answer, the one I'd learned. You went out with a gun to make your dreams come true. But it wasn't no good telling her things like that.

It was a couple weeks later I got an idea. It was when I was sweating over my books. I had a lot of figures to keep straight and they were getting more of a pain every day. Things like the daily take on the Italian lottery and who owed me what on the stills and accounts on shylocking and stuff like that. Big Sam was willing to help, but he didn't have no head for doing sums. And I didn't want nobody else knowing too much about my personal business.

Then I thought of Teresa. I made a point of going around to the flat when I knew Vito was busy elsewhere. I sat in the kitchen and drank a cup of coffee with Teresa and the old lady. I said I wasn't hungry but I ate a piece of pizza to be polite.

Finally I got around to what I had in mind. I spoke American, which the old lady didn't understand too good, so the conversation between me and Teresa was private.

"You've always been saying you're looking to do me a favor."

"You know that, Tony."

"Then maybe you can prove it. I got some work I can't handle good myself."

I told her what it was and how much it was worth to me. Sixty bucks a week.

"You ought to be able to do it in a couple of hours a day easy. That would leave you enough time on your hands to go to college, did you want."

She gave me a long, straight look.

"I was afraid that was what was on your mind, Tony. You can hire all the bookkeepers in the city for twenty-five or thirty dollars a week. I told you before, you've already done enough for us."

"This is different. I don't want no damned jerk asking questions I'd rather not answer. And sixty bucks is less than I have to pay flatheads that can't even run errands straight."

"Like Vito?"

"I ain't mentioning names."

Even so, it wasn't until later, after she got a look at the books and figures I was talking about, that she got sold. But she let me know she thought there was a catch.

"Now you've got the whole family living off you. Why, Tony?"

"Forget it. Nobody ain't living off me. I just like keeping my business with people I know."

Lessen she or anybody else should get ideas, I made her do the work at home. I didn't want her sitting in the office back of the barbershop with all the hoodlums coming in and out, making wisecracks or thinking things.

I wanted everything strictly on the up-and-up.

You had to be careful that way in our neighborhood.

CHAPTER TEN

IKE I say, the whole business was getting a bad name. Too many stupid killings and too many show-offs like Legs Diamond and the Dutchman and even Capone himself out in Chicago. It was clear that sooner or later something would have to give and there would be a blowoff.

Already it was in the wind. The word was out that the federals were looking for a way of cracking down. They couldn't get none of the big shots for stuff like boot-legging or mob killings because too many of the cops and agents themselves were mixed up in the racket.

Then some bright boy down in Washington thinks up the income-tax dodge.

It was Lepke who tipped me off what to do. He had a couple of boys on his payroll that could make figures do tricks and then Joe Santoro brought me a lawyer that was an expert in tax matters. Before they got through I had myself four different corporations. I called the pin-ball machines amusement novelties and set them up in one company. The one-armed bandits got called mint vendors. For a time I didn't know what to do about the couple hundred kitchen stills I had out, and then one of the tax experts decided they were household appliances that I rented out. So they went into a third company. Finally I had a real-estate and development company for dough I couldn't account for no other way. Everybody went on the payroll legitimate including even me and it was all tidy and legal.

I had the seals and corporation papers from Albany to prove it.

Lucky came around for a meet one day and I told him what I was doing.

"But why?"

"Lepke tells me there is tax snoopers going around checking up on things. If they find out you ain't been paying in the right percentage they can slap you in the can."

"You mean it ain't enough we've been paying off the local law? We got to start cutting in the government too?"

"That's what they say."

It didn't make no sense that you had to bust a half-dozen laws to make a buck or two and then when you had made it had to hand part of it over to the government for telling you you shouldn't have made it in the first place, but that was the way it was on the books. The law kept telling you that crime didn't pay and all the time it kept living fat off crime.

I used to get thinking about it sometimes at night when I couldn't sleep, but all I ever got was a headache. I never could find the answer.

It wasn't long after that the word came in from Chicago that the government was on Capone's tail for holding out on his profits. And the next thing anyone knew there were guys with brief cases and cheaters popping up all over New York asking questions and writing figures down.

But by then Lucky had seen the light and got the Unione affairs in order the same way I had done mine. It always gave me a tight feeling in my stomach every time I sat down and signed a check to the government for their split. I wasn't hiring no gang of sharpshooters to chisel down on what I should pay, like some of the big business guys I was reading about every day. I was giving the cut they said I should, strictly on the up-and-up. Yet that didn't change matters any—according to their say-so I was still just somebody out of the underworld, the scum of the earth.

There wasn't nothing wrong with my dough, though.

It was along about this time that we called a meeting to see if something couldn't be worked out to clean things up and bring a little law and order into the business. I'd had a feeling that a break was coming our way if we were smart enough to be ready when it came.

It was in the cards that come the end of Prohibition a lot of the mobs that had been powerful up to now would have tough going. They didn't know nothing but boot-legging and strong-arm stuff. When the booze money stopped coming in they'd wind up fighting among themselves for the leavings.

I figured we ought to stay out of it and kept saying as much.

"We don't want us wops getting a bad name. So far Schultz and Waxy and them jerks have copped all the headlines. Let them go on doing it and killing one another off. Then we can start things with a clean slate."

"The Dutchman's already trying to set himself for the future. The word is out he's moving in on the numbers racket in Harlem."

"So what? The dinges won't take it laying down. There'll be plenty of killings before he gets organized. Let him take the blame for them."

"Then what do we do? Sit here and just starve to death?"

"We go legitimate. We get things lined up so we can handle gambling clear across the country. Suckers will be betting on the horses or buying lottery tickets until hell freezes over. We move in on the unions and show them how to organize so everybody can make a buck. We get into the end that controls things, like right now we got our fingers on the plant that makes the slot machines. There ain't no end to what we can do, do we get businesslike."

There was a lot of batting ideas around, with everybody afraid to give up something they didn't rightly have for sure. Trouble was, we weren't all the same. The boys from Detroit, that was called the Purple Gang, was mostly Jews. The wops was strong in Cleveland and Canton and Columbus. Philadelphia was like New York, so mixed up that nobody knew from nothing.

It was Lepke who did best at talking. He had the figures to back up what he was saying and on top of that he could point out to Bernstein and the others he was a Jew who had done all right playing along with the Unione.

"We're talking among ourselves now, not to some politicians who would double-cross us the first chance they got. If we don't start by trusting one another we'll never get anywhere. It's the way this country was founded, a lot of little states getting together to protect themselves and form one big one."

That was Lepke. He read books and knew what he was talking about. You couldn't help but have respect for a man like that.

So in the end we come to kind of a loose agreement. Every outfit would be boss in its own territory. There wouldn't be no chiseling in or stepping on one another's toes. But on certain things that were national we would pool up. Right now there was rum-running, to give an instance. The Detroit and Cleveland boys were getting their stuff down from Canada and we were getting ours from over in St. Pierre. Sometimes the market was flooded and there was a price war. We'd dump what we couldn't use ourselves in places like Philadelphia and Pittsburgh. Other times you had hard work laying your hands on a bottle of the real McCoy quick. On top of that, every mob was having to pay off all down the line to customs men and coast guards and the sheriffs in the counties you rode the stuff through.

It wasn't good business. Anybody that could add two and two didn't need no argument to see that. Then there were other things. Some of the boys did business in narcotics and that was the same as the rum deals, with the market up and down all the time and too much throat-cutting that didn't do nobody any good. There wasn't any central gambling office, either, where the different city bookie outfits could lay off bets at the last minute when odds were too heavy, so things could be straightened out at the track.

One way or another there were a lot of angles to be worked out. It would all take time.

But we had made a beginning.

I've seen mention of that meeting since. You'd think from the way they tell it that we were plotting to blow up the country or something instead of trying to quiet things down so every side street wouldn't be a shooting gallery. That was something the cops hadn't ever been able to do during ten years of Prohibition. They had their excuse—they said they were letting the hoodums kill one another off. But the lives ones were good for a grafting buck, which is why they never flung none of them in the can.

We was always going to have rock-heads who thought the only way to get a buck was by going out with a gun. Just like there would always be punks looking to kill somebody to prove they were men. But that was human nature and we couldn't change it none.

All we could do was make rules for our own people. Rules they either had to stick to or get their head knocked in. There wasn't going to be any more imitation Capones rolling around in armored cars sticking machine guns out at everybody. There wasn't going to be any more killings to get splashed all over the newspapers. Everybody was to act orderly and like a gentleman.

Naturally, if some bastard kept getting out of line and figured he could do as he wanted, steps would have to be taken. But it would be done nice and quiet, without no body left in an alley for the cops to stumble over. There was plenty of deep water around about and cement was cheap.

You couldn't have no kind of orgainzation unless you had respect for your rules.

That was the way things were when Prohibition came to an end. There wasn't any quick change then, because for a while only beer and wine was legal so there was still a few bucks to be made peddling hard stuff.

But it was in the books it couldn't last long.

The way we'd predicted, most of the big-shot mob leaders that had been copping all the headlines for the past five, six years now began getting the kind of attention they didn't like. The federals was digging up laws nobody ever heard of before and putting the bite on guys like Waxy and the Dutchman and other for a million bucks up. Dough they'd maybe once made but sure as hell didn't have any more. And even could they come up with it, it wouldn't do no good because they could get slapped in the can for not saying they had it in the first place.

So the squeeze was on for more money. The Dutchman figured he could get it from the numbers racket up in Harlem. Up to then policy had always been strictly a dinge operation, something for no place but the black belt. But in those days the Dutchamn was paying heavier than anybody else for protection, and the way the story went it was the politician who did most of the business with him who steered him onto the racket.

On the surface it looked easy. The boogies wouldn't have no more protection no matter how much they offered to pay. It would be the Dutchman who had the green light from downtown in City Hall. All he would have to do was move in and take over.

Only it didn't happen as simple as all that. The dinges didn't want no white folks moving in on what they figured was rightly private stuff. There was a lot of killings and the kind of trouble that don't die down quick before it was over.

Even then the Dutchman had more of a headache than he knew at the time.

So while the other mobs that didn't have no real background were knocking themselves out trying to keep going, we took things quiet and stuck to spreading out in legitimate ways. There was plenty to do in just the labor racket alone once we got started. The new movie operators' union was working out real smooth and it showed the way. There'd been a little trouble at first, with the old union throwing out picket lines and even trying some rough stuff, but that was quickly taken care of. When it came to strong-arm business we had all the answers from way back. Likewise a lot of the independent movie houses didn't want to sign up right away but they changed their minds when they found people don't like going into a place that is likely to be filled up with stink bombs any minute.

After that everything worked out fine. A lot of guys had work that hadn't had it before, because we didn't charge any five hundred bucks to join our union. A C note was all it cost. And a whole flock of neighborhood show houses were saving a few bucks a week, only not as much as they thought they would, because we kept putting the bite on them for this thing and that. We'd go to them and say the operators were talking strike and it would cost money to keep the lid on and they'd come up with a wad of expense dough. But like Lepke said, it was only right that the sons-of-bitches should pay for being so greedy in the first place.

We started figuring other things then, and that's when I got to doing business with Red Nolan again. I'd kept up with him, doing him favors every now and again ever since the days when I sent him a few bucks out to the reformatory. He'd worked as a bartender during Prohibition and then had his own speak for a while. I let him get into me every once in a while for a few cases, knowing I wouldn't get paid off in nothing but promises and hard-luck stories. He wasn't no kind of a businessman and he'd still rather fight than eat. But he had a way with his own people.

I thought about him when Lepke and I were talking up a new union. Lepke had the kind of mind that thought things way out, seeing angles that nobody else ever noticed. Out of a clear sky he said to me, "Did you ever think what keeps a city alive? What keeps it going?"

"People."

He shook his head. "They'd all starve to death if it weren't for one thing. Someone has to bring in the food they eat. Just like somebody has to carry goods to and from the factories or they'd all have to close down."

I waited, not certain what he was driving at. Sometimes when he was talking his eyes got a dreamy, faraway look and I used to think that had things been different he would have been an artist, the kind that paints pictures or makes statues like Joie the Bug's older brother that worked for the gravestone outfit out in the Bronx.

So I waited and finally Lepke came up with his own answer. It was transportation.

"Think it out, Tony. Think what a union of truck drivers and teamsters would mean. Just in itself it would be powerful enough to toss a monkey wrench into the works. But suppose we had a half a dozen other unions, even small ones such as we've got now, and they were all tied into a working agreement. Then when we call a strike in the garment section or the produce markets or anywhere else the truck drivers and teamsters work with us. We'd be in the position where we could lock out the bosses instead of the other way around."

I didn't need for him to say any more. I could see. It was the kind of idea that is a natural—so simple you wonder why nobody ever tumbled to it before.

It was when we got to talking about the men we could use to front up the union that I thought of Red Nolan. There was a lot of wops driving trucks but we could handle them all right. Only there was a bunch of Irishers as well, and for them we needed the kind of mick who could talk their language.

The outcome was I fixed up a casual meet with Nolan. At first he thought I done it to put the squeeze on him for some of the dough he owed.

"I'm looking around to open a new bar, Tony. I've got a following and this time I'll make money. You'll be the first man I'll settle up with."

"Forget it."

He gave me a blank look. More than fifteen years had passed since I first tangled with him as a kid, but in lots of ways he was the same. Always looking as though he was too big for his clothes, with his shirt front gaping open over his pants. His face was a lot fuller than it had been back in the old days and splotched with red, like he'd swallowed a couple of stiff hookers of cheap booze too quick. Maybe he combed his hair in the morning or sometime, but it never looked it.

"You always were a friend, Tony. But I'll make it right with you."

I shook my head. "Why don't you face it up, Red? You ain't never going to pay me back from running no bar." I started to tell him he didn't have the head for it, was he given all the breaks in the book, but there ain't good sense in kicking a man you're figuring to use. Instead I spread a little oil. "There's going to be too much competition, Red. First thing you know, every jerk in town will be opening a bar."

"I got friends."

"So what? They'll wind up putting drinks on the arm. What you need is a new racket."

"I could get on the cops for a grand."

"Ain't one in your family enough? I know just the spot for you. All you'll have to do is talk and move around places. A hundred bucks a week and maybe more later."

He wanted to know what and I told him. Being president of a new union of truck drivers and teamsters. In the beginning he didn't even begin to get the idea.

"Christ, Tony, I'm no teamster. I don't know one end of a horse from another."

He didn't have to, I told him. Starting tomorrow he would have himself a job driving a truck for one of the wholesale markets downtown. It was one owned by a top member of the Unione, but I didn't tell him that.

"You won't never have to get in that damned truck lessen you want to take a joy ride. But it will make you eligible to join the union. There's mostly wops in it now and it will be up to you to talk in the mick drivers."

"How's that make me head man?"

"You'll get elected. I've got friends in the union who will take my word that you're the right man."

Even then he didn't have no clear idea what it was all about. Maybe it all sounded too good to be true. I could see him turning over in his mind the thought of being head guy of something and then he wanted to know what was the angle.

"What are you getting out of it Tony? I owe you over two grand and it will take a hell of a while to pay you back out of a hundred a week."

"Forget it, I told you. I just like to do a pal a favor."

"You're a real friend."

"Sure," I told him. "I'm everybody's friend."

I didn't bother to explain that in a union the president don't mean nothing, that it's a guy called the executive secretary that handles all the real important things. Likely he wouldn't have understood anyway.

Not then, at least.

That was close to twenty years ago, yet I still get a sour feeling in my stomach when I think of it. I wish it had never happened. I wish I'd never started him on his way. Most people in the know think I was smart for picking a winner out of nowhere and backing him right along into power. The kind of power he has today. We made money during those years, more money than there had ever been in the old bootlegging days. For a time we had everything sewed up, right up and down the line.

But I don't think of those things when I think of Red Nolan or see his name in the paper where he's swinging his weight in this or that labor dispute. I don't think that but for me he'd likely still be stuck behind some bar down in the Gashouse District, his flat feet planted in the beer slops.

All that comes to my mind is the way he turned yellow when the chips were down. The way he turned his back on Lepke, who along with me done most to build him up.

That's when I curse the mick bastard's name and spit on the floor. A man without no goddamned loyalty. A lousy politician at heart.

He should have been a cop like his brother.

CHAPTER ELEVEN

Money was tight along then, in what later the newspapers called the first years of the depression. Half the country was out of jobs and there was even soup lines over on Times Square.

It was a time that was full of headaches and it got me mixed up in politics more than ever. What happened was the city had to start shelling out relief to keep the people from getting so damned hungry they'd start busting in store windows. That was all right, but pretty soon the jerks hired to handle the setup began acting like it was their own dough they were handing out. It was bad in my territory, where maybe half the old-country people didn't speak no American and if they did couldn't see answering a lot of personal questions. They didn't like no strangers snooping all over the place, asking how much this and that cost and who was working and how much did they get.

I got hold of Santoro and our district leader and laid it on the line.

"Get the hell down there and lay the law down. We want our own investigators for this neighborhood, not a bunch of god-damned brown noses."

"It's supposed to be nonpolitical."

"Listen, you tell the main guy this whole stinking ward will be nonpolitical come next election lessen he plays ball."

So we eased in some of our own people, but even then it wasn't all easy going. They had too many rules. Did a family own a radio or a beat-up car or maybe somebody making an extra buck here and there, it was like they were related to Rockefeller. All the time, day and night, there was somebody coming to me to put in the fix for them and get them straightened out. It got so that every morning pretty near Santoro would have to stop by my office behind the barbershop and I would give him a list of names to take downtown to the reliefers.

It was a headache but it was like in the old days when I was spreading stills around and getting kids out of the hands of the cops. It all added up to votes, the only language outside of money the politicians ever understand quick.

Like I say, legitimate money was tight. Most of the bars in the slum neighborhoods had to keep cutting prices to hold their trade, and before long you could get a slug of whisky for fifteen cents, two for a quarter. That meant there was still a demand for raw alky, because the bar owners had to start mixing their own rotgut to meet the competition and make a nickel. By that time I owned a piece of two, three saloons in the neighborhood and I made them lay off stuff like that. It wasn't honest, and besides, I didn't want no reputation as a cheap chiseler. I made them hand out straight stuff over the bar even did we lose money or just break even.

In other ways things wasn't so bad. Always when a lot of people are out of work gambling picks up right away. When times are flush it don't mean much to a guy to win a couple of bucks on a horse or maybe a small lottery prize. But when there's no pay envelope coming in every week it's a different matter. Then squeezing out a few pennies to put on a nag or buy a lottery number is all that counts—it's the only hope there is of getting a break. People that ain't got nothing have got to have something to dream about.

So things were all right as far as the take went from the hand-books and the Italian lottery and the pin-ball machines. We got a break in labor organizing at the same time. It's easy to sign up a guy that's out of a job. You don't need to sell him no bill of goods. He's ready for anything different from what he's got, which is nothing.

The bosses helped, too, particularly the small ones over in the garment district. They figured that with so many out of work they could start cutting wages all over the place.

Lepke showed them different.

Maybe they could have got away with it in the old days, but not now. It didn't do them no good to call in a bunch of strike-breakers, did the union call a walkout. They were dealing with us, only they didn't know it, and we passed the word that any hood that did more than draw his day's pay would get his head knocked off. Next thing the teamsters would hold a meeting and pass a vote not to cross no picket lines. That meant no goods going in or out of the plant. From then on the sweatshop owner could sit in his office and chew his fingernails off. There wasn't nothing else he could do.

Sooner or later somebody would give him the word and he'd get smart and send for Lepke. Lepke or me, depending on were they Jews or wops we was dealing with. What happened then depended. Was it a big outfit, maybe all we did was insist they should recognize the union and stick to minimum pay rates, plus what we felt was due for settling the strike peaceful. Was it some smaller place where there weren't enough workers to make it important to the union membership, we would maybe do different. Usually it was the owner himself who came up with the bright idea. He'd start crying that did he run a union shop he'd go broke and have to close up. It would be worth money to him just to be let alone to run things his own way. Finally he'd name a figure.

We'd let him sweat for a while, telling him all the different ways it took dough to buck a union. Then we'd start coming up with other things. Likely he was busting the law nine kinds of ways in how he ran his place, without the right kind of safety precautions or water closets or any other damned thing. Everything he wasn't doing cost money.

It was all added up into the final figure that we took for calling off the strike and letting him run like he always had.

A long time later, when Lepke was on trial, a lot of those same bastards got up in court and yelled about extortion. How they had to pay off because they were scared not to. Truth is, the sons-of-bitches were only paying up because they figured it would be cheaper.

We was giving them protection to run the kind of lousy sweatshops they wanted. I still don't see where it was against no law. If it was legal for them to hire a bunch of hoodlums to beat up their strikers, it ought to have been just as legal to hire us. More so, because nobody got hurt our way. But the law said no. They've always got the cards stacked against you when they want to crack down.

They had passed another law that nobody who had had anything to do with bootlegging could get into the legitimate liquor business. That didn't mean anything much as far as bars and night clubs went. There was always plenty of guys around with clean records to front for you, and happy to make a buck.

But there wasn't no dough in that kind of penny-ante trade. The bars didn't mean no more than a living for one, two guys, and the only way you could keep most of the Broadway night spots going was by running a clip joint.

The real take was in the breweries and distilleries, the same kind of trade we had handled back in the old days. And in a way the new law was a break for it forced us to go on being businessmen whether we wanted to or not.

That was where the crew of Wall Street sharpshooters I had met through Rothstein came in handy. They knew all the tricks about setting up dummy companies and then turning over most of the stock to another phony setup and then putting that company in hock to a third outfit for a loan that was only on paper. By the time they got through it would have taken an army of snoopers a year to figure out who owned what.

That way we managed to get hold of a couple of breweries without nobody being able to put up a squawk. When it got to hard stuff it was another matter, because most of the distilleries weren't for sale and right then there wasn't no quick way we could bring pressure on them.

That was when we got to thinking about all the stuff we'd been importing over the years from Canada and England and Scotland. There wasn't no law to keep us from doing business direct with those companies, buying a piece of the outfit where we could and in others getting an exclusive agency contract for some dummy company we had set up. We had two good talking points. One was cash on the line. The other was the fact that did we turn thumbs down, their stuff would have hard going getting into the bars and night clubs in most of the big cities.

We could do that on account of the national tie-up we had worked out at the meeting in Atlantic City the year before. All we had to do was pass the word and the boys in Cleveland and Detroit and Chicago and all the places between would give out the orders to the saloons and night spots. It showed what co-operation would do. If you used your head you didn't have to go out with a machine gun to get a break.

It was a funny thing during those years of the thirties. Every time they passed a law that was supposed to put what they called gangsters in their place once and for all, it worked out good for us. Like the new mayor they got in the city who decided he didn't want no part of pin-ball games and slot machines.

Joe Santoro came back to me with the word.

"He ain't kidding. He called in the top brass yesterday and laid the law down."

"They've laid the law down before. Mostly it means they want a bigger cut."

"Not this one. He says he's going to run the goddamned underworld out of town."

"That will be the day."

But he wasn't fooling none about the machines. He not only had his picture took for the papers busting up a couple, but he began loading all the machines the cops could pick up onto garbage scows and sinking them out in the bay.

So we had to figure out something new. First off we had to find another territory to plant the machines to take the place of New York. Next we had to dope out something to keep the boys busy that had been working on the pin-ball routes and to help meet the weekly payrolls.

We got a break on the first angle we weren't even looking for. That was when the governor out of a southern state who was nine kinds of a rumpot landed in town on a drunk. He run up tabs in all the night spots on Broadway, including the one I had a piece of, and the word got around he figured he was a wise guy.

It was clear he was wide open for a deal.

We made a meet with him one night in the office of my night club when he was still sober enough to talk business. The proposition was a simple one. We'd set up a corporation, all legal and everything, just to handle the slot machines and pinball games in his state. He didn't even know if they were against the law or not, but if they were he agreed to put the fix in.

In return, all we had to do was give him 20 per cent of the take. There wouldn't be nobody else to pay off—no cops or sheriffs or politicians. Just him. Twenty per cent.

He gave out with a lot of high-sounding talk about how his end was going into a special charity fund to buy shoes or schoolbooks or some damned thing for the poor kids out in the country. Maybe he was kidding himself or maybe he even believed it. I seen a piece in the paper once how he was always giving a handout to the back-country folk he come from. But I took a trip down there once to check up on some race-track handicappers we had and I didn't see nothing but barefooted kids out in the hills. And if they had a schoolbook they likely used it for toilet paper.

That deal gave us the idea that maybe other governors had an itch for steady side money. After a while we formed a regular pattern. Come a few months before an election, when campaign money was tight, we'd send a contact to the top party men to make a deal. Always before the payoffs for gambling and suchlike had started at the bottom, with city police and county sheriffs, and worked their way up. We just reversed what had gone on before.

We had a good argument.

"There's always been gambling, but up to now just the cops and cheap politicians have been getting rich letting it ride. The main guys like you only get the rap when things go wrong and something breaks in the papers. Why not get smart and hand out the take yourself?"

There weren't many who were as raw as Huey Long down in Louisiana, who wanted to do it personal, but a lot of them had a friend in the shadows who could act for them.

And it was all laying the groundwork for easing in other things later.

I ought to have felt good about the way things were breaking, but always there was a kind of empty feeling. Once I had looked forward to the time when I would be on equal terms with the real big shots, but now that I was dealing with congressmen and senators and even governors I found it didn't make no matter. Understand they was the same as the first cheap grafters I had tangled with as a kid. Always with a hand out. Only difference was they cost more and you had to watch them twice as close.

You had to watch everybody, far as that went. Even friends— you. had to be careful who you let hang around with you. It wasn't so much that they would maybe get wise to too many things and double-cross you, but like as not they would start using your name in the wrong places and in the wrong way. First thing you knew you would find you were the pressure guy behind some racket you never heard of.

Too many guys were already using Lucky's name. I tried to warn him once or twice but he just laughed it off.

"So what? It don't do no harm everybody knowing you're important."

I couldn't see it that way. There wasn't any percentage in taking a chance on trouble that wasn't paying you off nothing. And on top of that I had an idea that the way things were shaping up spelled bad news. Everything was breaking too smooth, and when that happens the boys get careless. They begin to take everything for granted, forgetting all the work that went into building up the right kind of protection all along the line.

Even Lucky was getting fancy ideas. He'd taken to living in a crazy layout up at the Waldorf that cost a mint and acting like we already owned the country.

I still had the flat over Chico's barbershop. I had a couple of closets full of hundred-and-fifty-buck suits and twenty-buck shirts and stuff like that. The best that money could by. But sometimes I wondered what the hell else I had.

Once in a while Big Sam got to asking the same thing.

"Jesus, Tony, you don't never give yourself no break. What's the point of having dough if you can't have yourself a time with it?"

"You want I should start being a sucker at the races?"

"There's other things. Dames, to give an instance. You don't never give them a tumble no more."

Maybe he was right, I got to thinking, so every once and again I would get a bunch of dames out of the club or some musical show and we would throw a party. Never in my place—I didn't want them stinking up everything and spoiling it for after. I would hire a couple of suites at one of the Broadway hotels this mob or that owned, where it didn't make no matter what happened.

Big Sam was always happy such times. Give him a roomful of babes and plenty to drink and it was like he never grew up. He never got it clear in his mind that it was the hundred bucks a night the dames were playing up to.

Trouble was, I always got to thinking at the wrong time. It didn't do no good reminding myself of how far I'd come from the slum roofs, the way Big Sam was always doing. Buying Angie a couple of sodas down to the corner candy store wasn't no different from giving some Broadway dame a century note. Except that the way I remembered Angie was more modest-like.

Next day I would soak out four, five hours in a Turkish bath and wonder what the hell was wrong with me. Always such times, without wanting to, I would get to thinking about Teresa. She was still doing my personal books and going right along in college, the way she wanted. I'd see her most every evening when

I dropped around to the flat to take some figures or check up on this and that.

Once or twice I had her and her old lady around to my place. The first time the old lady moved around touching everything, like she couldn't believe it was real. Teresa was quiet for a long while, just looking.

"You did all this yourself, Tony?"

"That's right. Why? Ain't nothing wrong, is there?"

"No. Everything is lovely. Your—your friends must think you have good taste."

"What friends? I don't use this for no hangout. I keep it private."

She looked at me again, long and straight, as though she was trying to figure something out carefully.

"How about all your lovely show girls from Broadway, Tony? Don't you ever give them a break?"

I didn't like her talking about things like that and said so flat. "They ain't for you to dirty your mind with, understand? You got other things to think about now."

She gave a queer-sounding laugh. "You forget that I'm a big girl now, Tony. And besides, I was born and brought up in this neighborhood. That's an education in itself."

"That don't mean you can talk like no goddamned bum."

"I'm sorry. Forget it, Tony. Forget I spoke."

Then her old lady cuts in. She can't understand what we're saying because it's in American, but she can tell there is an argument. So she begins in Sicilian, trying to smooth things over.

"A woman you should have, Tony. All this place without a woman is no good for a man."

Teresa got red in the face and turned on her sharp, telling her she should keep quiet.

"For why? What do I say? It's natural a man should have a woman."

There wasn't but one way to stop the talk. I went over and turned on the phonograph and got out some Caruso records, him singing *Pagliacci* and *La Bohème* and all the stuff nobody but him could ever do right. I had some real Lagrima Cristi from the old country and some cakes that weren't too sweet to go with it, and it was nice sitting there listening and having the right kind of company.

It was living human, almost like the way I'd figured things would be someday.

But Teresa had the last say. It was when she and the old lady were saying good night.

"You've got a beautiful place. Only don't you ever get lonely, Tony?"

"You kidding? They don't leave me no time for stuff like that."

"What do they leave you, Tony?" she asked softly. "Did you ever think of that? What do they leave you?"

Maybe she didn't expect no answer. She had shook hands, real formal-like, and turned her back before I could think of one.

CHAPTER TWELVE

I WAS RIGHT when I said I didn't have much time for being by
myself. I was trying to shape things up in a solid pattern and it
wasn't always easy. I could see a clear outline of the way things
ought to be, but there was always somebody wanted to do it different, wanted to go back to the old days.

So I had two things on my mind always. One was how to
keep spreading out all over the country, getting power in the
places that counted without attracting too much attention. The
other was keeping my own district in line.

Because by now there were guys coming up who had ambitions to take my place. Rock-heads who wanted to give orders
instead of taking them. They figured they didn't have to take
nothing off nobody, that they could build their own little mobs
and do as they liked.

On top of that, what with the depression still going on,
there was a lot of punks had an idea they could make an easy
living in the underworld, where they didn't rightly belong to
begin with. Two or three times I had a showdown with Lucky
over it.

"These bastards don't do us no good. We ought to kick them
all back into the gutter where they belong."

"We came from the gutter, Tony."

"But we didn't bring it with us. These jerks ain't got no respect
for organization. They belong in a jungle somewhere."

"Let the cops work on them. We got other things to do."

But it was a mistake. All along I kept telling myself that. It was a mistake. We was businessmen now, and except for the muscle boys we had to have to keep our rules enforced or maybe bring some outfit into line, we shouldn't have no hoodlums messing things up.

On top of that, every once in a while there was somebody looking to knock you off for no reason you could find out except maybe they didn't like the way you ran things. A couple of times coming home late at night there was quick shots thrown at me.

And then one early evening when I was coming out of the building where Teresa lived I nearly got it.

Seemed like something hit me before I heard the shot even. I was halfway down the brownstone steps when it happened and I went the rest of the way like one of those dreams where you are falling off the top of a building and can't stop yourself. Afterward I figured it was cracking my head against the sidewalk that knocked me out.

It was bad because I didn't know what was going on and result was the cops and their goddamned ambulance got there before my own people could take care of me.

I come to down at Bellevue with croakers and plain clothes dicks standing around. Seems like they'd dug a slug out of my chest somewhere and wanted to make a big play out of it.

The cops started talking soon as I got one eye open.

"Who did it, Tony?"

"Who did what?"

"Don't be a wise guy. Another half inch and you'd have been drilled through the heart. Come clean, Tony. Who did it?"

"How should I know?"

"Lay off that crap and start talking. Don't think this is something you can handle yourself. There's not going to be any new gang war busting out."

I felt too tired to argue. The sons-of-bitches were just talking big for the croakers and the newspapers anyway. Making something out of nothing.

"I want my lawyer and my own doctor. You bums can get the hell out."

There was more words but I didn't bother to listen. I had things in my own mind to work out. I couldn't figure but a couple of people who knew I was going to by where I was when I got put on the spot. One was Teresa, but that didn't make no kind of sense.

Then there was Vito, her punk brother.

He'd been hanging around the flat when I got there instead of being out checking up on juke boxes, like he was supposed to be doing, and I'd sent him on his way. He hadn't liked it none, but he never liked taking orders.

But I couldn't figure him with guts enough to try the job himself.

After a while I give up thinking. There were other ways of finding out without batting my brains out in a stinking hospital room.

Big Sam came to the hospital along with Santoro. He was all set to start busting things apart right away did I tell him where to begin.

"Maybe now you'll believe me, Tony. You ought never to go nowhere without a couple of the boys tailing you."

"I'm living, ain't I? Maybe if there'd been more shooting I wouldn't be."

He had the same questions to ask that the cops did, but he was smart enough to clam up when I gave him the eye. Later I would set him to work moving around, seeing what he could hear and pick up in the right places. That was one reason I had wanted my own doctor.

"Give out the word I got hit bad, Sam. Make it like I'm going to kick off. Then watch which guys get to bragging too quick."

That was sometime around two or three o'clock in the morning. The doc gave me a shot of something to make me sleep, and when I woke up again Big Sam was still sitting there.

"What the hell's the idea? I thought I sent you out to do things."

"I been out. This is another day, Tony. You been conking off for eight hours nearly."

"O.K. So maybe I needed the sleep. You find out anything?"

He didn't know whether he had or not. There was a rumble that a new mob was forming up in the neighborhood that wanted to make a name for itself overnight, but so far nobody was admitting being in it.

"The way I figure it, we got some rats in our own outfit, Tony. Let me find out who they are and they won't be around long."

"We'll find out," I promised. "Take it easy. We'll find out."

Then he came out with something else.

"That girl Teresa has been after me all morning. Vito's sister. She was all for coming up here with me."

I tried to sit up but couldn't make it.

"Tell her to keep the hell away. Ask her does she want her name in the newspapers or something? Tell her I ain't seeing nobody—most of all her."

"I'll tell her, Tony. I'll tell her. Don't get yourself all excited."

"I ain't excited. I just don't want no dames busting in here."

I tried to get him to blow then but he wasn't for leaving until a couple of the boys came to sit with me. He kept reminding me of how guys had busted in on Johnny Torrio in a hospital out in Chicago once.

"You couldn't protect yourself none was you alone. You ain't even got a rod on you."

I grinned at him. "They didn't shoot no holes in my head, Sam." I slid my hand down under the sheets and came up with the flat Luger I kept for personal wear. "What the hell you think I had Santoro up here for?"

It was four days before I got out of the hospital and back to my own place. By then I had plenty to do. Nobody could put a finger on the new mob that was maybe in the making. It was like as if everybody as sitting quiet waiting for the other guy to make the first move.

And there was something else in the wind. It was one of those goddamned cleanups the city was always having to make some new headlines for a few politicians. Only this time something got out of hand and the first thing anybody knew a special prosecutor had been appointed and what they called a blue-ribbon grand jury set up to hand out indictments like they was relief tickets. Then the word got around that it was the Republicans upstate that was calling the shots and what they was after was to stink up the Democratic machine in the city and they didn't care who got thrown in the can.

It was Santoro who got the inside dope. He wasn't a city councilman any more but a state representative and he had pipe lines into the right places.

"They ain't going to be able to sidetrack this guy Dewey. He's got too much power behind him, pushing him on."

"Can't he be reached?"

"Not from where we're sitting."

So the outcome was we had another meeting. Not in New York, because by this time we'd been tipped off there was stoolies and wire tappers working all over town. We didn't have nothing to worry about, but there was no point in anybody getting ideas.

We held the meet down in Atlantic City, like before, and we spread out all the information we'd been able to pick up one place and another. We'd been shoveling money like it was horse manure down to Centre Street to get as near an inside track as possible.

Santoro give out first with what was known for sure.

"Right now he's out to get Jimmy Hines and bust up the Dutchman and the numbers racket in Harlem."

That gave Lucky a laugh.

"So what? He'll be doing us a favor both ways. When he's finished we'll move in and take over."

"Maybe you will," Santoro said slowly. "Maybe. But I hear he's out to get you next."

Lucky looked surprised and hurt.

"Me? I ain't done nothing. What the hell has he got against me?"

"Maybe he don't like it you live in a hundred-and-fifty-bucks-a-day suite on top of the God-damned Waldorf and wear silk drawers," I told him. "What's it matter what he thinks he's got? I told you before he was bad news, Lucky."

That wasn't all of it. Seems like Lepke was on the list, too. The way it looked, Dewey was figuring like he was a hero in the moving pictures, out to clean up everything in sight. Doing what the cops and the federals hadn't never been able to do did they feel like it.

"He's nuts!" Lucky kept insisting. "He's just blowing off to sound good. There've been others like him before."

I had a feeling it wasn't going to be that way. I'd made a point of getting a good look at him once, and I didn't like what I saw. And I'd heard things—mostly that he had been promised that if he made a name for himself he could go places.

So I had my say.

"I don't hold with knocking guys off needless, but sometimes there ain't no other way to protect yourself. This guy is bad news.

He's young and he ain't got no money and right now he won't take. But he's ambitious, and an ambitious politician is ten times worse than the cheapest grafter. That kind will double-cross their own grandmother to make a record."

There was a lot more words without us getting anywhere or deciding anything. Lucky and Lepke kept holding out that Dewey wasn't nothing but a quick flash and in the end wouldn't mean much. Besides, knocking him off would cause too much of a stink and make him look more important than he was.

So in the end we took a vote and Luciano and Lepke had their way. It was to lay off and take a chance on what would turn up.

"If he turns the spotlight on us we may get some bad newspaper stories but that's about all," Lepke decided. "He can even indict some of us for some charge or other, but that isn't a conviction. After all, what have we got lawyers and courts for?"

That was a question I was to ask myself later on more than once. Just as I was to remember that it was Lepke and Lucky who gave the green light for Dewey to go ahead without his ever knowing it. Without his ever knowing how near he came to being just another name on a tombstone instead of something that hits you in the eye every time you open a newspaper.

I went back to making my own plans in my own way, trying to protect myself from every angle I could think of. That is all you can do when you feel trouble ahead—make yourself solid in the right places so that if they start gunning for you legal they will find they're hitting too many important people.

When they had run the slot machines and pin-ball games out of town I had to find something else to take their place and keep some of my boys busy. Juke boxes, these stinking machines that play what the jerks call music, was the answer. The factory we owned out in Illinois could turn the damned things out and see to it that they only went to members of our syndicate scattered across the country. That's what we called ourselves now when we spoke of the national tie-up we had. It sounded better than saying the mobs.

I handled all of the city for my own personal take, and to make it look right I set up another corporation. Only this time before I did so I called in Joe Santoro and we did some careful planning. There was always judges and different police officials who had close relatives who were foul balls when it came to making a living, and they would be happy to see them set up in a real business.

When we got through we had four dummy officers with the names and right family connections that would be drawing a salary just for thinking they were in business. But it was worth it. Did somebody start an investigation sometime, nobody could see the juke boxes was gangster-controlled.

I did the same thing every other way I could, too, trying to keep myself as far in the background as I could. I didn't like the way Lucky was setting himself up to get a lot of the wrong kind of publicity. His name was beginning to pop up in the papers too often and always they gave in big round figures what the take was he was supposed to handle from the underworld.

It was up in the millions somewhere.

They never did bother to say what the expenses for running an organization like we had ran to. The way they wrote you'd think it was all profit.

Same time I was having a mixed-up kind of argument with Teresa. Rightly speaking it wasn't an argument, it was just that all at once she started having ideas of her own and whatever I had to say didn't seem to mean nothing.

It started over my giving orders she shouldn't come to the hospital when I was there.

"It wouldn't have done any harm, Tony. There's nothing wrong in your having friends that worry about you."

"You want the cops and newspapers knowing you're mixed up with goddamned hoodlums? You want them on your neck every time something happens?"

"I can take care of myself."

"You ain't acting that way. I did what was best. Forget it."

She was quiet for a minute, then she said slowly, "They were saying you wouldn't live, Tony. At least you could have sent word that it wasn't so."

I didn't say anything.

"Was it because you were shot coming out of my place? Is that the reason you've been acting so strange?"

"I haven't been acting no way. Forget it," I said.

Only she wasn't for forgetting it. Maybe she had the same thing on her mind I did.

"Vito—" she started, then stopped short, looking at me straight.

I pretended not to understand. "He giving you trouble?"

"That's not what I started to say, Tony. And you know it."

"Stop talking riddles!" She had cornered me in the office behind the barbershop, where I'd told her not ever to come. "Go on, get out of here and go home. Big Sam will be bringing you over the books later. I got a meet here with somebody and I don't want no dames hanging around."

She took her time about going, in the way women have when they want to show they can do as they like if they have a mind to.

At the door she stopped and said quietly, "Don't try to be tough all the time. You don't have to pretend with me. Not ever."

"You're nuts," I said. "Get out. I got things to do."

After she was gone I tried to figure out what had happened, how it was that she could be calling the turn the way she was and not me.

I didn't like not being sure of things. I didn't like not being able to put things in their place and keep them there. I had decided long ago where Teresa belonged as far as I was concerned.

She shouldn't be getting ideas of her own. I hadn't no time for worries of that kind.

I had other worries.

As far as New York went, the heat was on. Dewey was raising nine kinds of hell, starting with Hines and the Dutchman in an attempt to throw the book at them on account of the numbers racket. And that was when the two of them began collecting on the enemies they had made when they took over the black belt. There was dinges aplenty only too ready to go downtown and spill all they knew to the special grand jury Dewey had set up. The way they figured it, they weren't ratting on their own people but on some sons-of-bitches that had moved in and taken over.

I'd seen what was coming and made my own contacts here and there with the right parties up in Harlem. It was clear that when the Dutchman got busted the whole policy business would be wide open. That was when money and protection and organization would count. I had all three. And I had an idea that the numbers needn't be just a dinge operation but could be spread out all over the city.

Then the word got around that the Dutchman was threatening to tell too many things did he have to take a rap. And there was another story going around that he was trying to collect all the loose cash he could and take it on the lam, leaving everybody else holding the bag.

He started hiding out over in Jersey, trying to run things from there. It didn't do no good, though. Nobody was surprised when the end came, lessen it was the Dutchman.

Even so, it was bad shooting. It took a long time for him to kick off in the hospital, and nobody felt real easy until the word came that he was dead.

He wasn't no gentleman, anyway. Just a bum you couldn't trust. Nobody was sorry to see him go.

So I had the new policy business to think about and divide up territory on. That took time and plenty of work. I had to set up regular business offices in hide-aways, with adding machines and telephones and guys that were good at doing figures fast. I had to pick the right men to be collectors and assign the sections where they would meet the different runners, the ones who picked up the individual number slips to begin with. It would have been easier if I could have had just one big central bank, but instead I did the same as I had been doing all along with the handbooks for the races, setting up a lot of branch banks. That way if one got knocked off by some cops out to make a record it didn't make no great matter.

There was another national election coming up and I began laying out heavy dough in the places it would do the most good to get Santoro on the ticket as congressman from our district. Having a smart man in Washington who was really one of our own would help in plenty of ways. Just money alone wouldn't do the trick, though. Votes, or something that sounded like votes, was needed to make sure the political bosses wouldn't try to pull any double cross at the last minute.

So I called in Red Nolan and laid the law down.

"Call a meeting of the union and pass a resolution that Joe Santoro should be the next congressman from this district. See that the boys make plenty of noise so they can hear them all the way down to the White House."

"Santoro? Christ, Tony, most of my men never heard of him."

"So what? They never heard of you before I put you in the damned union."

"Don't get me wrong, Tony. I'm not giving you an argument. Hell, whatever you say goes with me. Only you ought to have let me know before."

"Why?"

He began hedging. Then it came out that some of the micks from Tammany had been giving him a little oil about being a faithful party man like his cop brother and supporting whoever they said to support.

I listened long enough and then cut him short.

"That's their story. Now I'm telling you what to do. Come out for Santoro and come out loud."

"Sure, Tony. Anything you say."

It should have been a tip-off then that the bastard was going to get too big for his britches in time. Then and there I should have cut him down while he was still just one more labor punk that nobody would have missed long. But I had too many other things on my mind. I let it ride.

A mistake.

Right then things were shaky anyway because Dewey had started after Lucky. The cops were using that as an excuse to jack up their demands on graft and protection money, the way it always happens when there is a cleanup campaign going on. It cost more money to operate every time you turned around and you wasn't in no position to spit in their faces the way you felt like.

Lucky kept saying they couldn't touch him for nothing and for a while it looked like he was right. He went off to Hot Springs for a meet with some of the top boys from the other mob's around the country and was willing to bet that by the time he came back everything would have blown over.

Then a crazy story started going around that didn't make no sense. First we thought it was just some junkies talking, trying to set themselves up to make a touch or get in right. Because the word was that Dewey was lining up evidence that Lucky was heading up a goddamned white-slave racket.

Any other time it would have been a laugh. Maybe Lucky had dealt in a lot of things, at one time or another, but he hadn't never peddled no dames. For one thing, he couldn't have done it and headed up the Unione, because the Unione didn't have no time and no use for pimps. Sure there were wop pimps, just like there were wop cops and wop sons-of-bitches, but they weren't never taken into the Unione. On top of that there wasn't no big dough in trying to control the whores in New York. No dough and too many headaches. It was strictly stuff for jerks that didn't have the brains or guts to get a living no other way.

That was what Dewey was fixing to pin on Lucky. On the face of it, it was a rap that was a cinch to beat. But I had a talk with Santoro, who was smart about such things, and after I learned a few things I wouldn't have wanted to make no book on it.

"Sure, Lucky's got the law on his side," Santoro told me. "All the law that's in the goddamned books. They haven't any legal evidence against him. But when it comes to a trial none of that will count."

"What the hell you mean it won't count?"

"Not in front of a jury it won't. Facts never do. By the time Lucky gets up in court you won't be able to find twelve men to sit on a jury whose minds aren't filled up with all the junk they've been reading in the papers."

"That still ain't evidence."-

"They'll have it. You ought to know by now that they never have any trouble getting a certain kind of evidence. They've got plenty of trained canaries to sing any way they tell them."

And that was the way it worked. They got two-bit whores off the streets and junkies that nobody in a decent mob would trust to go down to the corner to get a newspaper. They got a couple of jerk wops that had figured to make an easy buck living off a flock of dames. The same kind of flat-headed hoods I had warned Lucky about when they started using his name too free around town.

It was the kind of evidence Santoro had said it would be.

"I saw Luciano once in a restaurant talking to the man who threatened me if I didn't work for him."

"They told me it was Lucky's orders."

"Everybody knew who the head man was."

"It was the Maffia.... It was the Unione.... It was the man they called Lucky Luciano...."

It was a stinking nightmare. None of it added up. Sometimes it seemed Lucky was being tried because he lived in the Waldorf and wore fifty-buck hand-painted ties. Or because somebody said the underworld made a million bucks a month or a week or a day. The figures kept changing. Some old bag said she had to take on thirty, forty customers a day at two bucks a throw and they made it sound like she was maybe paying Lucky's rent personal.

I didn't need to wait until the end to know what the answer would be. The only question was how much of a bit Lucky would get, for it was clear they were fixing to throw the book at him. And that meant he'd be out of circulation for a long time.

Other parties would be having the same thing in mind. It meant there would be another rumble inside the Unione, with one person or another looking to fill Lucky's shoes. It was in the cards that some of them would be figuring to do it the old way, at the point of a gun.

That was the way it had always been in the past, but now I was fixing to use other weapons. I had been a long time in learning—a long time in building up and planning for just such a time as now.

From here on out I wasn't going to be second fiddle to nobody. It was going to be just one.

CHAPTER THIRTEEN

I T WAS a lot different than in the old days.

Back before when there had been a scramble for top place the planning had gone on in back rooms somewhere. I did my work down in Santoro's law office and across town with the head of the bank I'd been dealing with now for nearly ten years. I was doing business the way I'd studied to do it from Lepke and Rothstein and the other smart operators. Only I didn't figure to play it too smart, like Rothstein. He woke up dead one day, he was so smart.

It paid off now that I hadn't never thrown my dough around just to prove I had it but had stashed it away in property and the kind of government bonds you can always raise a buck on. It was even better that all along I had made a point of getting loans from the bank when I didn't need them. I had good credit now when it counted most.

For there were things I wanted that were going to take plenty of ready cash. I wanted to latch onto the stock in the joint out in Illinois that turned out the slot machines and juke boxes. I wanted to take over Lucky's end in a couple of breweries. And I wanted to have the kind of bankroll that could finance everything else like the policy racket and the gambling combines did I have to do it independent for a while.

Then there was the graft—the protection money. Lucky had been handling it before, but now he had other things on his mind.

I took over.

Big Sam didn't get it at first.

"Jesus, Tony! Shelling out dough all over the place. It ain't even certain yet who is going to take Lucky's place."

"I got an idea."

Big Sam didn't say nothing for a couple of minutes. Then he let out that he'd been hearing things here and there. Mostly about Frank Petrucci.

"They're talking him up in some places, Tony. But maybe you already heard."

"I heard, but it don't mean nothing. Not yet."

Frank Petrucci had been in the Unione a long time. He wasn't no big shot, but he always acted like he ought to be. Maybe he would have been if his cousin Mike hadn't been rubbed out for bucking Joe "The Boss" Masseria in the days when Masseria was fixing to take over.

Almost I had to think twice to remember it was me that had pulled the trigger on Mike. It was long ago and a lot had happened since then. On top of that it had been nothing personal that would stay in my mind. Just business.

But it was in the books that maybe somebody would figure to do the same to me. I was too close to Lucky and the top. There would be parties that would want me out of the way permanent.

Frank Petrucci was one. Then there was Cherry Nose, who had run the kid mobs when I was coming up from nothing. Cherry Nose was another who hadn't got no place after his brother Mike was wiped out. He'd always been around, talking big and doing nothing.

And there were others.

It was all something I would have to handle when the time came. But until then I had other things to do. It meant taking trips to Cleveland and Detroit and Chicago, and then down to Florida and Louisiana. Talking to the top men in each mob that was a member of our syndicate. Laying the cards on the table with facts and figures.

I had the things that counted. I was the big voice now in the factory that turned out the slot machines and juke boxes. I could call the turn on who got the output of two of the biggest breweries in the East and who handled the best of the imported whisky. I had the central bank where the different city mobs could lay off heavy bets on the tracks or if certain numbers got too much of a play.

I had the right political connections in a dozen states and even down in Washington. Connections I'd been building up and paying for over the years.

It all added up to the kind of argument that makes sense. Did they want a businessman or a rock-headed gunman to take Lucky's place? That was all. Was they nothing but hoodlums or had they learned to use their brains?

I got some arguments but not many. The windup was that in most places I got a go-ahead providing I could handle my own territory and swing it into line.

It was when I got back from a meet out in Chicago that Big Sam gave me the news that Joie the Bug had been picked up on a narcotics rap.

"I ain't surprised. He's been asking for it for a long time. Can we make a deal if he cops a plea?"

It wasn't that simple, Big Sam told me. Joie hadn't been picked up by accident but nabbed cold, like somebody had put the finger on him. On top of that, certain parties were spreading the word around that I couldn't protect my own people no more, that I was getting too big-time to bother with small stuff.

"Who's saying it?"

"Frank Petrucci. Cherry Nose. Guys that hang around with them. And something else. They know things about your business that are strictly private."

It took a minute for it to sink in, to get what he was driving at. Then I asked careful, "Any ideas?"

I could see Big Sam didn't want to answer, but he had to. That was the way he always was—honest even if he figured I'd jump down his throat for it.

"That dame Teresa that's been doing your private books all along. They got plenty in them."

"So? You standing there telling me she's turned rat?"

"Jesus, Tony, I ain't telling you anything. The books is at her house. She's got that punk brother Vito who ain't no good to nobody. I'm just reminding you of things, Tony."

I took it a little easier then. It made a picture. Vito. He was a dirty little rat who couldn't be trusted to do nothing but something stupid.

"Tell me something, Sam. You had an eye on Vito recent?"

"I keep an eye on everything when you're away, Tony. You know that."

"I'm asking about Vito."

"I always told you, Tony. He's no good. He's been hanging around with Cherry Nose and that mob recent. And one more thing. He was all of a sudden getting thick with Joie the Bug for a couple of weeks before Joie got nabbed by the feds." He stopped as though thinking out careful what he had to say next, then added flatly, "It was in a private drop nobody but Joie's friends knew he had that he got picked up."

I could take it from there. It didn't make any difference whether Vito had turned stoolie because he was a yellow double-crossing punk to begin with or because Cherry Nose or somebody had put him up to it to make things look bad for me. The harm had been done. Now I had to settle it.

First off I had to spring Joie. I would have liked to let him rot in the can for a while to get some brains in his head, but now it wouldn't look so good. It would look like what they were saying was true—that I'd got too big for my own people.

They had him up for a hundred grand bail, like he was a real big shot. It looked better in the papers that way. They had found maybe ten ounces of junk in his drop, which had cost about two grand to begin with. But you'd never know it from the newspaper stories. When the feds gave out the story they figured what the junk would bring cut down and adulterated and split up into about a thousand decks an ounce and then peddled for a top price. A half-a-million dope haul was the way the papers read.

So first off I had to start bringing pressure here and there to get the bail cut down and Joie the Bug out on the street. Then I had to look for some way of putting the fix in.

It wasn't easy with the heat that was on in New York. It was a federal case but that didn't make no difference. Most of the men in the D.A.'s office I had done business with said flat they didn't dare touch it.

"There's been too much of a play in the papers, Tony. This is just one of those times when nothing can be done."

"Don't talk stupid. Something can always be done." Then I got the beginning of an idea. "You got any objections to postponing the case a few times?"

"Your man's lawyer can always get sick."

So next I got hold of Santoro on his next trip back from Washington. I knew what I wanted. It was a list of the federal judges from the different districts and which ones were scheduled to sit where. That is a system the federals have. They got their permanent judges in each district but some of them visit around regular from one part of the country to the other. What I wanted to know was when one of them was coming up from one of the states in the South where my slot machines had been paying for the governor's liquor and women for the past four, five years.

After that the way was clear. I had the name I wanted and I got on a plane and went to handle the business personal. I started with the governor and talked the only language he could understand well.

The windup is he calls in the judge that was scheduled to sit up in New York in about five months.

There was a long song and dance when he introduced me, about how I was a businessman with heavy financial interests in the state.

"He has a personal problem, Judge, The young son of old family friends of his is being railroaded to jail by dirty Yankee politicians."

"I see."

"He can arrange it so that you will hear the case when you are sitting up in New York next spring."

"I see."

He turned and looked me over. He was an old bastard with white hair fluffed up like a ham actor's and a black string tie in a bow around his collar. There was a couple of spots of coffee on his shirt front and he smelled of whisky. The way he looked at me, I got the idea he didn't like wops or no kind of foreigners. A real Southern gentleman.

It was clear he was waiting for me to say something, so I made the usual speech.

"It looks like an open-and-shut case, Judge, but you can't judge by appearances. This unfortunate boy just got tangled up with the wrong guys and they left him holding the bag."

"I would have to know a great deal more about the case to venture an opinion."

"He's already told you, Clem," the governor cut in smoothly. "Did I mention that Mr. Mauriello was one of the biggest contributors to my private charities? A real humanitarian at heart. He can always be depended on, Clem. Always. You only have to take his word for what's right."

The Judge cleared his throat. He stared at the two of us hard like we were a jury in some courtroom. "I am sworn to uphold the integrity of the court, gentlemen. That, sirs, is the glorious tradition in which I was reared. But true justice must always be tempered with compassion and understanding. I pride myself that I have both qualities." He stopped and cleared his throat again. "You might get that bottle of private stock out of your desk, Gene, and offer us both a small libation."

They was fancy, high-priced words, but they came down to meaning it was in the bag.

Twenty-five grand it cost me in the end for the governor's goddamned private charities.

It was just something I had to do to show I was still boss, that I could still swing weight in the right places at the right time.

When Joie the Bug finally come up for trial, he copped a plea and got a suspended sentence of one year.

But there was still Petrucci and them that took orders from him to handle.

And Vito.

I decide to tackle Petrucci first. I ain't for waiting for him to start no more rumbles. He's just rock-headed enough to start a crazy gang war and I ain't for having no killings. Such thinks looked bad in the papers, particularly with Dewey still making a noise like he was fixing to head up the twelve apostles.

So I arrange a friendly meet in a spaghetti house. We talk about the frame they've laid on Lucky for a bit and then I get to the point.

"I hear you got ideas of filling his place, Frank."

"I got more than ideas."

"Like putting the finger on some more of my boys, maybe?"

He don't like that. He got red in the face and spat out some wine. "Don't call me no goddamned rat. I don't have to sit here and take that talk."

I didn't say anything. I just sat there while he kept on cursing me and then while he got up and started for the door. We was sitting in one of the two private dining rooms of the restaurant, and when he got to the door he found out why.

Big Sam was there, blocking the way.

"Slap the bastard back in here, Sam. Any of his mob hanging around outside?"

"There was a couple, but they been taken care of."

He was slapping his hands over Petrucci while he talked, and then he ripped the bastard's shirt open in front and pulled out a gun that had been tucked under his belt and tossed it to me.

"I'm surprised at you, Frank," I said. "This was supposed to be a friendly meet."

"You go to hell!"

"After you, Frank. Now, what else you got besides ideas makes you think you can step into Lucky's spot?"

Friends, he said. Plenty of guys that didn't like the way things had been run the last few years. Guys who would do what he told them with no questions asked. To hear him tell it, he had everything.

I got tired listening.

"Crap!" I said. "That's what you got. Horse crap. Get wise to yourself, Frank. This ain't the old days. It takes more than a couple of guns to run things now."

"You won't be around to prove it."

"I'll be around. You want to know for why? Because you nor no son-of-a-bitch like you will be no place without me. Without me there won't be no easy dough around, because I got everything tied up. Tied up legal, Frank, like you own your own building legal. The slot machines and juke boxes and breweries. The dough that finances the shylocks and the bookies and the numbers. You knock me off and the whole goddamned underworld outside a handful of hopheads like yourself will be looking to blast you because the whole racket will be busted wide open. That's why I'll be around, Frank."

"That still don't say you can't be rubbed out."

"They'll bury you the same day. If they can find enough pieces of you to put together in a box."

I didn't want no more talking. I give Big Sam the nod and got up.

"You want I should take care of him, Tony?"

I shook my head. "Give him time to think and pass the word around. Maybe he'll wake up to himself does he live long enough."

So then there was Vito.

I was of two minds what to do. I checked with Big Sam and found that Vito hadn't been showing in his usual hangouts since Joie the Bug had been nabbed. Same time Teresa let me know that he hadn't been around home too much.

It wasn't hard to find out he was still sucking around Cherry Nose and Petrucci and the rest of their little mob. Finally I sent word I wanted to see him.

I fixed the meet for late at night in my office behind the barbershop. I was sitting there reading a tabloid spread out on the desk when Big Sam passed him in.

I didn't say anything for a minute, just looking at him. He was dressed sharp, like the wise guys that hang out on Broadway, and he kept fidgeting with his shirt cuffs and the knot in his tie, which was the size of a baseball.

When he couldn't stand the silence no longer he broke the ice. "You want to see me?"

I shook my head. "No. I don't never like having to look at yellow-bellied rats."

"You got me wrong, Tony."

"I ain't never had you wrong. What give you the idea you were smart enough to start pulling a double cross?"

"I don't know what you're talking about."

He began turning sulky. I was watching his eyes as they shifted around, and the pupils were small like little black beads. I knew then that he'd turned junkie and that he'd given himself a bang before he showed up.

"I'm talking about your new pals. Petrucci and his gang. Joie the Bug that you likely put on the cuff for junk and then fingered for the feds. All the other rock-heads you're hanging out with. That's part of what I'm talking about."

"I pal up with who I like. You ain't running my life."

"I say different."

I had been talking quiet, the way I always tried to do. Yelling don't get you no place. Maybe that's what give him courage. Or maybe it was the shot in the arm he'd taken. He starts raising his voice and shouting and spilling things because he got drunk with his own words.

"I don't give a damn for what you say. You ain't so smart as you think. I don't have to take no crap from you ever. I know too much, see? You ain't been getting away with nothing while you been playing around with my sister. You're going to start paying for it and paying plenty. And I work or not as I feel like."

I kept hold of myself. All through the years I'd learned the hard way to keep hold of myself until the right time. I let him keep spilling words that came out like spit from his mouth. I let him start calling me names and following up one threat with another when I didn't answer back. Telling the private stuff he'd found out by sticking his nose in my books when Teresa wasn't around. Getting more and more hopped-up courage as he went on.

All the time I was thinking in the back of my head how he was Teresa's brother. But that couldn't be helped. I'd told myself that a dozen times—it couldn't be helped none whose brother he was.

Even so, that was why I was seeing him personal now, handling things in my own way.

He was born to die young. That was all. How it happened didn't matter.

He give me a headache talking even though I wasn't listening to his words no more. I cut him short sudden.

"You packing a rod, Vito?"

He stopped with his mouth half open, staring at me blankly out of those pin-point eyes.

"You shouldn't never talk that way without a gun to back it up," I said softly. "It ain't healthy, Vito."

His hand started for the inside of his coat then. They're all so goddamned smart, carrying their guns in a special pocket built in the left side of their coats, thinking the fancy handkerchief they wear outside is going to cover up the bulge.

I'd kept the tabloid open on my desk all the time I was listening to him shoot off his mouth. I had my hand underneath it now, around the butt of the little flat .32. I didn't bother to move the paper. At that distance it was like pointing your finger. You couldn't miss.

His gun made a noise when it clattered down on the floor. More noise than he made himself. I had to get up and walk around the desk and look down to see where I had hit him. There was a lot of blood and I wished I'd thought to put a cheap rug down first.

Big Sam had swung in when he heard the shots and was standing with his back against the door.

"Anything wrong, Tony?"

"No."

He moved Vito's head with his foot, watched it fall back on the floor,

"Where you want him put, Tony?"

I'd already figured it out. There was an empty beer barrel in the back hall that had been sitting there since who knows when. I told Big Sam to get it.

I emptied Vito's pockets. He had a roll of dough that was too much for what he had been knocking down from me and a notebook filled with dames' names and phone numbers. He had a ring with a diamond that was a phony. Inside the bottom of one pants leg he had a little pocket with a folded packet of white stuff in it. It was heroin.

He fitted neat into the barrel and we got the barrel head back on so it would stay put. Then I sent Sam over to the garage to pick up a panel truck.

While he was gone I smoked a cigarette and wondered why it was sons-of-bitches like Vito had to always foul things up. I thought how it would have been easier for me if I'd never gone to bat for him in the past. By this time he'd likely have burned in the chair or anyways been up the river for life. I should have let the law handle him from the start.

Big Sam came back and I told him what I wanted.

"Pick up a couple of the boys and drive out to City Island. Load the barrel on Salvatore's boat and fill it up with rocks. Drop it in the Sound somewhere up off the coast of Connecticut. If you get going you can be done by daybreak."

I helped him roll the barrel outside. It was early March and there had been snow during the late afternoon that had turned to rain. Now there was a thin coating of ice on the sidewalks and we kept slipping around.

I didn't hear nobody coming until a voice spoke up right behind me.

"They got you doing an honest man's work for a living now, Tony?"

I looked up. It was one of the mick cops on the beat. I answered him before Big Sam could do anything.

"Something special for a private party. Somebody slipped up and I'm handling it personal."

"It's a cold night to be drinking beer."

"Get some exercise and you'll warm up."

He gave us a hand swinging the barrel into the truck. I wondered if he knew how much a kegful of beer ought to weigh. The goddamned thing didn't even smell of beer no more.

I said, "Thanks, Casey. Get yourself some whisky around at the bar. Tell them I said give you a bottle of my private stuff."

"A gentleman you are, Tony. I always said so. A fine, understanding gentleman."

"Sure. That's what the mayor is always saying."

He pounded on down the street and around the corner. Big Sam was swearing under his breath and I told him to save it.

"Get going. And if the boys should ask you, you don't know who the hell you got in there."

I went back into the office and looked at the floor again. In the morning early I'd have to slap some paint around to cover things up. Then I walked upstairs and fixed a hot bath. I turned the dial on my radio till I got some opera music and felt the doors open into the bedroom and bathroom.

I sat in the steaming tub a long time, listening to the music of Donizetti and trying not to think of Teresa.

She and her old lady would be better off now, anyway.

CHAPTER FOURTEEN

S O NOW for a while everything started breaking smooth. Everybody was saying how Dewey had busted up all the rackets in New York and nobody thought to ask how the hell they had got to operating so big in the first place.

Lucky and a couple of other guys had gone up the river but the same grafting cops were around. The same grafting cops and the same money-hungry politicians and the same goddamned slums that were like a jungle.

Nothing had changed. Just a lot of newspaper headlines and a couple of top men taking the rap because the world was crooked to begin with.

The heat went off once Dewey had made his reputation. The only difference was things had to be run quiet and businesslike, the way I had been talking up all along. I'd been fingered two or three times when he was trying to build up a case against Lepke. They tried to say I was behind half a dozen different rackets, what they called a power in the underworld. But they couldn't prove nothing. I was a businessman and had the legal papers to back it up.

A businessman, but without none of the breaks other businessmen had for nothing. Did I need legal protection I had to pay for it cash on the line behind a closed door somewhere and it got called another name. Let one of my collectors get smart and start holding out dough and I couldn't run to no court. Or did somebody else owe me heavy money the law wasn't no good. I had to handle things my own way.

I could move out of the goddamned slums now because my district was just a small part of what I had to look after. I could let some of the boys that had come up with me through the years take care of things, with Big Sam to check up regular to see that they didn't get too far out of line.

I got me a big apartment on Central Park and fixed it up even better than the one I had so long over the barbershop. I took a suite of offices downtown on Wall Street, where all the big-shot businessmen hung out. I wanted to do everything right or not at all.

I had a long black Cadillac and one of the boys dressed up neat in a dark suit and dark tie to drive it. Everything on the up-and-up. Everything respectable.

I had plenty to do. Sometimes I wondered how it was I had so much to do. It was just me and a half a dozen men like me running things all across the country. Running what the newspapers and the double-talking politicians called the underworld. They didn't give us no credit for organizing things—no credit for setting things up so the guy with a couple of bucks could make a bet easy and be sure he was going to collect if by accident he hit it lucky. Instead of half a hundred little mobs trying to knock each other off over who would get what, there was just one big one now.

The Syndicate.

On my end I handled things proper. In the morning I rode down to my office and went over all the figures that had come in the day before. Figures from the bookies and numbers bankers. Reports from the slot-machine operators and juke-box combines. The same thing from the breweries and whisky distributors and every other thing we owned or controlled. It gave me a nice feeling looking at all the clean pages of neatly typed sums and checking off one thing against another. It was a hell of a lot different from when I first started doing business as a kid in the mouth of an alley off First Avenue, collecting from the pushcarts and paying off to the kid mob and the coppers on the beat. Different from running errands for the whores at Dirty Mamie's and peddling the stuff we lifted off the trucks to the fences over on the Bowery. It showed that a man could get ahead and make something of himself if he put his mind to it.

Come noon I rode uptown to Chico's barbershop and got myself a shave and a massage. In a way it was a second office, because here I met the different ones from my own mob who had things to talk over. Maybe more dough for the shylock business or an argument over juke-box territory or trouble of some kind among the bookies and numbers runners. And then all the other things that are always happening—things I had been handling now for damned near twenty years. Slum problems. This one after a touch and that one after a job and somebody else wanting a fix put in with the law. Every day they were waiting when I showed up. Even Sundays, when Chico opened the shop special just to take care of me.

I moved further uptown for lunch, to one of the small Italian restaurants in the East Fifties. There was nothing on the menu less than a buck and the headwaiter didn't let no jerks in. Nothing but high-toned society people that knew how to behave themselves. I had the same corner table reserved all the time, did I show or not, and I never had to ask twice for anything. I was as good as anybody else in the place or maybe better.

It was my dough that had opened the joint to begin with.

Late in the afternoon I had another regular spot. It was the cocktail lounge in a little family hotel off Park Avenue where nobody but old folks with so much dough they could afford not to show it hung out. It was here I made my meets with the judges and politicians and such-like that didn't want to be seen going in and out of my office downtown. It was here I made the important payoffs for fixes and connections. Nobody called me Mauriello around the place—it was always Mr. Murray. The manager of the hotel knew different, only he wasn't saying, any more than he was saying that it was me held the mortgage on the place.

Come seven o'clock and the car called for me and I drove home. It wasn't an empty apartment no more, the way it had been down on the East Side, because Teresa was always there waiting for to have dinner with me.

That was something I hadn't been able to regulate. It hadn't done no good talking, because no matter what I said she had an answer.

Only thing I never knew was if she was smart as to what had happened to her brother.

She had come to me about a week after Big Sam had taken him away in the barrel.

"It's about Vito again, Tony."

"What about him?"

"Mamma's worried. He hasn't been home in seven or eight days now."

I had been wondering all along what I was going to say when she came to me, as I was certain she would. And now she was in front of me and I still didn't have no clear answer.

"She don't have to worry about him," I said finally. "He won't be getting into no trouble where he is."

"How do you mean?"

I had to pick my words careful. "He got to hanging out with the wrong guys here. Sooner or later he'd have wound up in the hot seat. So I sent him on a little trip."

There was a silence that was almost too long before she spoke up. "Will we be hearing from him, Tony?"

I shrugged. "You know how Vito is. He don't never think of nobody but himself."

I could feel her eyes on me, watching me, and I could almost hear the questions she wasn't asking. At last she said softly, "Mamma wouldn't worry so much if she got word from him from time to time."

"She'll get word. I'll see to it personal she gets some kind of word."

She didn't say no more. I would have felt better if she had. I never liked not knowing what was in people's minds.

So after that every now and again I would drop around to her old lady's flat when I knew that Teresa was up at medical school and hand out some kind of story about hearing from Vito. And I would put some gills in her hand and say that Vito had sent the money.

"Only don't say nothing to Teresa about it. She likes being independent."

"You're a good boy, Tony. Always I say that. You got a big heart, all the time thinking of other peoples."

"Sure. Only keep it a secret. Ain't no good letting the whole world know it."

"Always making jokes, Tony. Everybody knows what a good man you are."

I would drink a cup of coffee with her then and eat a piece of coffee cake or pizza. With old-country people you got to be like that or they think something is wrong and you ain't a real friend.

I didn't want no ideas like that getting around.

All this time I was missing Lepke. Not just for business reasons but as a friend—somebody close I could talk to. Now Big Sam was the only one left I could trust. He was faithful like a dog and I thought more of him than I would my own brother, but even so he wasn't no good when it came to anything outside the rackets. The only music he knew was the latest corn the jerks were playing on the juke boxes and he never read nothing in the papers outside the sports pages and the comics.

Not like Lepke. With Lepke I could go to an opera or a concert like it was a natural thing to do. He read books and knew how to talk and behave. Always quiet and refined and never no rough stuff. A real gentleman.

But in the end it did him no good. He might just as well have been some cheap hoodlum out of the gutter like the Dutchman or Waxy or one of them punks the way they treated him.

For they got him like they did Lucky. They got him worse, for it was three kinds of a double cross all along the line. Maybe it would have been better for him if he hadn't beaten the rap Dewey tried to hang on him at the start. All that noise about extortion and using labor union to build up his power. Because when that didn't work they tried to find something else.

Like Lepke himself had said when they were framing Lucky, "There isn't any law any more. They can always beat you if they set their minds to it. We've got two strikes against us before we ever get up in a court, Tony. And they've got their own umpires to call the third one whenever they like."

It had just been Dewey that was after Lucky, looking to make himself a reputation, but with Lepke it was something different. That got clear as time went on and we got a tip-off from this party and that in Washington as to what the score was. It was politics again—the kind of dirty politics that is always going on behind the scenes.

What it boiled down to was that Lepke was too powerful. He had built up a couple of unions from nothing and now their leaders were big shots, walking in and out of the White House like it was a corner saloon. Red Nolan was one of them, and there were a couple of others. On top of that there were too many politicians that owed Lepke too much.

So the Republicans up in Albany were trying to grab him to put the squeeze on for what they could maybe learn, to show up the Democratic machine, and at the same time certain parties in Washington wanted to get hold of him to put him where he couldn't say nothing.

There looked like only one smart thing to do. Lepke let the word out that he had taken it on the lam and dropped out of sight. But that didn't help none. Fact was it seemed to make matters worse. Not being around he began to get blamed for everything and the first anyone knew the government had an indictment against him on a narcotics rap, which may have been legitimate and maybe not, and there was word the state was after him for some phony murder charge.

I saw him just before he decided to give himself up.

"Maybe I can make a deal with the feds and maybe not," he admitted. "But the worst that can happen is that I'll do a bit for a few years. When I come out they'll have something new on their minds and maybe will leave me in peace."

"If you're alive. When you give yourself up some son-of-a-bitch will likely get trigger-happy, figuring to make himself some headlines knocking you off."

"I've thought of that. I'm not giving myself up to any cops, federal or whatever. I trust the bastards as much as you do. That's why I've been thinking of surrendering to Winchell."

"The newspaper guy?"

"That's right. It will be like giving myself up in front of the whole country. No cop is going to be stupid enough to try to pull a fast one if it will hit the headlines of half the damned newspapers in the morning."

I didn't want to see him do it, but I didn't have no other bright ideas. And in the end that was the way it worked out. He gave himself up and took a rap three yards long from the government on the narcotics beef. They shipped him off to Atlanta and for a while it looked like he was safe.

Only it didn't work out that way. Like we had been learning the hard way from the start, you couldn't depend on no law. They rigged it up to suit themselves. According to the lawbooks and every high-priced mouthpiece in the country, there wasn't nobody could touch Lepke until he had served his sentence. Did New York want to grab him on a murder rap, or anybody else want him, they would have to wait until his time was up. They could wait at the prison gates with handcuffs did they like, but for the next ten years that was all they could do.

That's what the lawbooks said. But what happened was something different. Always it is something different when you can't depend on nothing. First thing anybody knew they were hauling him up to New York on the murder rap and then trying to find ways they could grab him from the federal pen and toss him on the hot seat up in Sing Sing.

Trying to do something was like batting your head against a stone wall. I kept seeing lawyers and political fixers and everybody else I could think of.

"There ain't nothing to worry about," they went on telling me. "He's safe until his federal bit is served."

"What the hell you mean, he's safe? He's in New York now, ain't he? They got him framed on a murder rap, ain't they?"

"The courts—-"

"To hell with the courts!"

So I seen Red Nolan. By then I was going around in circles, talking to myself half the time. Trying to do the things I knew Lepke would do for me was the deal the other way around.

Nolan was one of the big shots in the labor picture now and acting like he'd done everything on his own. He gave me the glad hand and started a lot of crap about how important old friends were.

I didn't have no time to listen to empty words.

"Cut it. This ain't no social call. It's about Lepke."

"And a goddamned shame it is. He was a fine friend in a good many ways."

"In every way. You know as well as I do that it's a lousy stinking frame they're pinning on him. It was some goddamned labor goon did that killing. Lepke never knew nothing about it."

Nolan shrugged. "You may be right, Tony. But thinking it ain't proving it."

I was certain then that he knew. I had a hunch that maybe he'd ordered the killing himself in the first place. There'd been murders before, when the unions was fighting one another, and Nolan would have known how to do it so that the finger would have pointed toward Lepke.

"Look, you mick son-of-a-bitch. Don't just sit there and give me words. Do something!"

"Jesus, Tony, what?"

"Get hold of the bastard that really did the job. Make him come clean."

"But I don't know who did it. I can't go putting my own boys on the spot."

"To hell with your boys. Your boys and you too."

"That's a fine way to talk to a friend, Tony."

"You ain't no friend. You ain't no friend to anybody but your own stinking self. If you were a friend you'd start using what pressure you got right now. Get the hell down to Washington and tell them you'll start rigging strikes from here to hell and gone unless they protect Lepke. You're a labor boss because we made you one. Begin acting like one."

"There's a war—"

"So what? What the hell's the point of having power if you're afraid to use it?"

Same time I was thinking what was the point of using words. I was just going around in circles, getting nowhere. Not helping Lepke. Not helping nobody.

The mouthpieces kept telling us it couldn't be done legal, but they did it. The federals commuted Lepke's sentence to time served, which meant the state could throw him in murderer's row up at Sing Sing. Still bringing pressure, still trying to make him talk. He knew too much about dirty politics, dirty labor rackets, dirty deals for this and that.

His friends—the men he'd helped in politics and labor and this business and that—turned rat and run out on him. In the end he was the only one left that acted like a man.

That was up in Sing Sing, where they kept hammering away at him hour after hour during the couple of days before he was scheduled for the chair.

"Tell what you know and a deal can be made," they kept pounding. "It ought to be clear to you what your friends are worth now. Why protect anyone who won't come to your help when you need it?"

He had an answer. "Because I'm me. I've lived according to my own laws—and one of them is that a rat doesn't deserve to live. I wouldn't want to live myself if I turned squealer. I could face men like you, perhaps, but not myself."

So he died the way he'd lived. Like a gentleman—the kind they don't make no more.

The night they pulled the switch was the only time since I was a kid I deliberately tried to get drunk. I still had the apartment then over Chico's, and shut myself up in it and kept putting Caruso records on the phonograph and turned it up loud. Like as if I could drown out my own thoughts. I had a bottle of good brandy and I drank all of it, sitting there listening and trying to keep my mind from working and my eyes off the goddamned clock that was ticking away the time. The time that Lepke had left to live.

It didn't none of it do no good. The music wasn't as loud as the words inside my head and the brandy might as well have been water.

It wasn't just that Lepke was due to die, but the stinking way he had to go. There hadn't never been nothing hit me so hard. Never.

And then the very next night Teresa lands in my place and insists on a showdown.

CHAPTER FIFTEEN

I THOUGHT at first she'd come on account of Lepke, knowing the way I was feeling, because that was the first thing she spoke about.

"I'm sorry, Tony," she said softly, putting her hand on my arm. "Words aren't any good at a time like this, but I wanted you to know I understand."

"Thanks, kid."

She had busted in on me unexpected up in my apartment, and now that she was there I figured it wouldn't be no harm if she stayed a while. I went and poured out a couple of small glasses of wine and then started to put another record on the phonograph.

She stopped me.

"No music, please. Not right now. We've things to talk about."

"I don't feel like talking."

"But I do. Did you happen to notice, Tony, that I have an overnight bag with me?"

I didn't get it. "So what? You going someplace?"

She didn't answer right away. I was standing by the table at the side of my favorite chair, taking my time picking a cigar out of the humidor, my back turned toward her. When finally she spoke up her voice was soft like a whisper but I could hear it clear because it was almost in my ear and I could feel her breath against the back of my neck the same time I felt her hands on my shoulders.

"I'm not going anyplace, Tony. Not away from here. Not away from you."

I turned around and it was a mistake because she was too close against me, too much a part of me.

"What the hell's wrong with you?" I started yelling. "You blowing your top?"

She stopped me with her lips against my mouth, her arms tight about my neck. I never knew before a woman could be so strong and so soft at the same time. It wasn't easy to break away and it took longer to get my voice the way I wanted it.

"Get out! Quit acting and talking like a goddamned whore and go home!"

"I am home, Tony. This is where I've belonged for a long time. I'm going to stay here tonight and every night."

"You want I should throw you out by force?"

"You wouldn't dare. I'll rip my clothes off and run up and down the street screaming you were trying to rape me. Try it and see. You wouldn't like that, would you, Tony?"

"You're a bitch!"

"Perhaps. But I'm a woman, and that's more important." She came close to me again and her voice went soft once more. "Stop thinking of yourself, Tony. I've been a woman for a long, long time now, Tony—a woman without a man. Without the only man I've ever wanted. Without you."

"It won't work, goddamnit! It never works for guys like me. Suppose I get in a spot like Lepke?"

She stopped me short. "Suppose you do? It was what happened to Lepke that helped me make up my mind. I'm not a weakling. Tony. I can take anything that comes. But if it does come I'm not going to regret all the rest of my life that I never had an hour's full happiness or love. I'm only half living now. I'm only half a woman until you make me whole."

Something snapped inside me then. Maybe it was because I was all broke up about Lepke. Maybe it was because deep down inside me I didn't have no real answer to the things she was saying.

"Goddamn it, you don't know nothing about me! You got no idea what I'm like inside. A cheap hoodlum dressed up in fancy clothes—that's all I am."

I slapped her then, hard and quick across the face.

"That's the way guys like me treat their women. You want to be some hoodlum's bitch now?"

She closed her eyes quick and then opened them, standing there without moving, not even moving when I slapped her hard again. She was wearing a plain blue silk dress and I crooked my finger in the neck and ripped it down the front and tore away the things she was wearing underneath, leaving her standing there naked in her stockings like a cheap whore.

All the time I was shouting at her, throwing back the words she had used.

"This is the kind of love you'll get from me. This is all that guys like me know—how to beat their dames up and get them into bed quick and then kick them out. That's the kind of happiness and love you'll get. All you'll ever get out of somebody like me!"

There were tears on her cheeks, like she was crying without making any sound. Not trying to move away when I struck her again. Not trying to protect herself, standing there as straight and proud as though she didn't know she was naked. Acting as though she couldn't hear the ugly names I was calling her, like as if my words was meant for somebody else.

It wasn't until I stopped at last that she finally spoke. Her voice was so low it was almost a whisper but I could hear it clear.

"Please, Tony. Please don't...."

I figured she'd had enough then, but I wanted to make sure. I wanted to end it once and for all.

"Please don't," I repeated back at her. "That's all you'd ever be saying with a guy like me. Begging me to act decent and getting slapped down for your answer. That's the kind of life you're asking for." I went over and picked up the coat she had been wearing when she came in and tossed it at her. "Get smart and get out."

She let the coat drop to the floor without making any effort to hold it. She just stood there, shaking her head at me, her voice soft and even. "You still don't understand, Tony. It's not me you're hurting, but yourself. Please don't try any more. Please don't...."

I couldn't find no answer. There weren't any more words in my mind, and then it was too late for words because she had come up to me and her arms were about me and her body tight against mine. I put my hands on her waist. Maybe I had thought to push her away. But instead my hands slid over her bare flesh, over the curves of her hips, locking her hard against me, against the demand I had always denied.

A long time later she turned to me in the darkness. Her voice was as soft as her fingertips, which had been moving so lightly over my body.

"Are you asleep, Tony?"

"No."

"I was asleep for a little bit. For just a little while I left you."

"Go back to sleep again, baby."

"Later." Her body turned against mine, warm and demanding. "Why are you so quiet, Tony? What are you thinking about?"

"You," I told her. "Thinking about you."

"Don't think now, Tony." Her parted lips were urgent against my mouth and the sudden tightening of her arms asked what she didn't know the words for. "There's time for thinking later."

I wondered what she would say if she knew for certain what had happened to her brother Vito. I didn't want to think of him but I couldn't help it.

I wished I hadn't had to kill the bastard.

Teresa stayed that night and other nights, and that was one of the reasons I took the apartment over on Central Park. I didn't want nobody noticing her coming and going from my place in the neighborhood.

There hadn't been no dirt touched her name ever, and I didn't want it to begin.

So now I had everything. I was sitting up near the top, one of the half-dozen real rulers. Everything I'd dreamed of as a kid and worked and sweated for over the years. Money didn't mean nothing personal no more—for a long time I'd had more than I could use. Now it was just figures on a sheet of paper, handy to swing deals with and buy power and protection. I was handling a lot of the Syndicate money, too, and I put it places it would do the most good. Legitimate places, like hotels in Miami and Palm Beach and in the gambling towns out in Nevada. I bought into race tracks here and there and got control of a couple of taxicab fleets. Things that would make money and keep the boys busy at the same time.

You couldn't stay boss unless you could take care of your own people.

The war years were kind of a rest, in a way. The politicians out to make a reputation for themselves were busy waving flags and there wasn't no percentage in them yelling about the under-world. So for the time being they let us alone and everything was nice and orderly, the way it should be.

I lived human. I liked driving down to the office in the morn-ing like any other successful businessman. I even had respectable callers now and again. Mostly it was when they were making some kind of charity drive and putting the bite on everybody. I always came up with a heavy contribution.

"Just give me a receipt to show the income-tax people," I'd tell them. "But don't use my name otherwise. Just put it down from a friend."

"Not everybody is as generous or as modest, Mr. Mauriello."

I'd shrug it off. "I ain't looking to be a big shot because other people need help."

They'd pass some more polite words and then be on their way after thanking me again. It made me feel good being able to hand out the dough, but the sons-of-bitches could have protested a little more about my not wanting them to use my name public. Jesus, you'd think they were ashamed the dough was coming from me.

I did other things. I spent a tough time learning how to ride a horse properly, but I never did feel comfortable on one of the damned things. But I did it so I could get up early and take some exercise in the park. You met some nice people that way. It was like a club—they figured if you was dressed right and rode right you must belong. Like the kid gangs back in the slums, where everybody had to be the same.

I bought me a place for the summer out on Long Island, right near Piping Rock, where the rich society people hung out. I met some of them, too, and even got an invitation to join a private beach club. But I turned it down. Sooner or later somebody might get wise that Anthony Murray who had an office down on Wall Street was Tony Mauriello the underworld boss, and I didn't want nobody getting embarrassed.

Besides, there was Teresa to think about. I wanted being with her as much as I could, but without it attracting no attention. I didn't want it known she was tied up in any way with me.

I wasn't for having her put in a spot where some smart cop could start putting pressure on her, did he want to learn something about me, or where maybe some rock-head hoodlums would be getting ideas they could get even with me for something by grabbing her.

Besides, she was a regular doctor now, with a degree and. a diploma and every other goddamned thing that went with it. She was doing work in different kid clinics in the slums, which was something she'd always wanted, and I wasn't letting it get spoiled no way.

I should have known it couldn't last. When things run peaceful for too long, guys get careless or big-headed, or fall in love with the limelight, like Bugsy Siegel was doing out west. First off he starts sinking a wad of Syndicate money in a hotel in the middle of some desert out in Nevada and then he starts throwing his weight around Hollywood like he was some movie star. And he began talking back when we gave him orders.

He talked back too goddamned much.

It made a stink when he got knocked off, with everybody's name dragged into the picture. The cops and newspapers started yelling about crime and the underworld, something they never bothered much about until somebody like Siegel got rubbed out. It was a headache.

On top of that it made things tight all over the place for a little while. Every time you turned around there was a different politician standing in your shadow with his hand out. They had a new racket now.

"There's a crime investigation coming up," they would let you know. "We're trying to keep it quiet so you won't get no bad publicity."

It got so that it cost more to keep your nose clean than it had in the old days when you were settling a fix for a murder rap.

Sometimes I got to wondering who the hell I was working for, anyway. New York wasn't supposed to have no gambling, for instance, but you could put a bookie in the middle of Times Square did you have a mind to and were you willing to pay the bite. That was all right. That was business. But what wasn't honest was the way the cops kept building up the squeeze. They weren't satisfied with fifty bucks a week a bookie any more. It was a hundred, then two hundred, and kept going up. Did you pull the bookies off the street and set them up in a flat or office somewhere to take bets over the phone it was worse. A bookie with fifty, sixty customers had to have three or four phones for when the races were on, to take last minute bets and stuff. The cops started tapping wires and pulling quick raids. It didn't mean nothing that couldn't be fixed, but it was a stinking nuisance. The only way out was to pay the law a set sum per month per phone.

They started in easy, asking no more than a couple hundred a month for every phone in a bookie's joint. Then the bite started creeping up until it got to a grand and a grand and a half.

As far as New York went, the law was making more dough than I was.

I wasn't any too surprised when a rumble started. It always happens when the cops get too greedy for their own good—other cops who ain't got the guts to get in on the take or are too stupid or even sometimes are honest enough to take their jobs serious begin spilling things to the wrong people.

So then there is another investigation hitting the front pages.

The last one happened just before election time, the way that the politicians that are on the outside looking in always plan. It got to be a game they was playing half across the country yelping about the underworld because they didn't have nothing better to talk about.

The first thing anyone knew, a bunch of senators down in Washington set up their own committee to investigate crime so they could keep their names in the headlines.

I didn't pay it no mind at the beginning. I'd seen it all happen too often before and knew how it would wind up. They might finger a couple of racket guys to begin with, but if they investigated too far they'd find they was digging up dirt in their own front yard and then they would have to work twice as hard having to hush everything up.

But I get burned up when I see the stink they are making because all of a sudden they discover that there is what they call underworld money in all kinds of legitimate business. They act like there ought to be a law against anybody being honest.

Once when I get hot under the collar I blow off to Big Sam about it.

"What do them bastards want, anyway? Used to be they'd blow their tops because there was an underworld with a lot of rackets they couldn't put their finger on. Now they're sore because we're legitimate businessmen."

"You want I should see some of them personal, Tony?"

That was Big Sam. Always willing to do anything but with only one idea about how it could be done.

I laughed and shook my head. "You can't strong-arm these jerks, Sam. You got to take your chances and let them get smart their own way."

But that didn't stop me feeling bitter. Jesus Christ, I was paying taxes, wasn't I? I was paying every goddamned penny the government had coming to it and maybe more. I wasn't taking no chance on laying myself wide open for no tax snooper. The businesses I controlled were run right, too. We didn't have no labor trouble and I never raised no stink about having to pay social-security bites or any other damned thing they asked for. During the war the juke-box plant and a couple of clothes factories had even turned out defense work.

What the hell more did they want?

They wanted headlines, that's what they wanted. Headlines and a couple of fall guys to take the rap. They started slapping subpoenas all over the lot and when you got down in Washington before the Senate committee they threatened you with a contempt-of-Congress rap if you didn't talk.

It was another frame like with Lucky and Lepke.

And my turn was coming. I knew it and Teresa knew it.

It was the waiting that broke Teresa. It was what I had always known would happen—why I hadn't wanted to ever get tied up close to no woman.

She started one night after dinner in the apartment when I had turned off the radio after listening to some news guy tell what they had done to a couple of the Chicago mob down in Washington. I made a crack about what would likely happen to me but she didn't answer right away.

It was two, three minutes before she said. "You don't have to wait, Tony."

"Wait for what?"

"For what they'll do to you when they get you on a witness stand." She was looking at her hands in her lap as she spoke, turning a big diamond ring I had bought her once around and around. When the stone was hidden by the inside of her hand it looked almost like a wedding ring. I was thinking of that instead of her words as she started in again. "You don't have to wait. You can quit any time you want to."

I didn't get it at first. "How do you mean, quit?"

"Everything." She leaned forward and her voice lost its cool smoothness and her words came out in a hot rush. "Quit everything. You don't have to keep on with the things you've been doing. You don't have to keep on giving your life to the mobs and the underworld and a dozen different rackets. You can stop any time you really want."

I gave her a hard look.

"You saying I should take a run-out powder?"

"I'm saying you've got a right to your own life. Oh, I know I promised never to talk this way, never to interfere. But I can't sit by quietly and see you sacrificed because half the country is corrupt. I can't do it, Tony!"

She was starting to cry and trying to pretend she wasn't. It made me sick deep inside to think I was to blame for it. I was to blame and there was nothing I could do.

"Goddamn it!" I yelled at her. "I can't do nothing else. I told you that a long time ago. I can't never do nothing else."

"If you wanted—"

"It ain't what I want. It's what they'll let me do. I'm legitimate now, never mind what I was a long time ago, but the sons-of-bitches don't want it that way. Like when I was a kid down in the slums and took a walk out of the district, there's always some lousy flatfoot to snarl, 'Get the hell back where you belong!' That's me. I was born in the underworld and they ain't for letting me forget it."

"You're wrong, Tony! You must be wrong."

"The hell I'm wrong!" I was shouting like an old-country wop now, forgetting all the years I'd trained myself to talk quiet and smooth. Forgetting all the dreams I'd ever had. "Read the papers if you don't believe me. Listen to the goddamned radio. I ain't no decent businessman. I ain't nothing but a hoodlum out of the gutter dressed up in two-hundred-dollar suits and silk drawers. I ain't no politician that's still a gentleman even if he lands in the can. I'm just the guy the bastards live off!"

She started to cry out something but I didn't let her finish. I didn't want her words loud enough so I would remember them later.

"How the hell do I quit? How, goddamn it? They're trying to drive me out of legitimate business because they don't want no competition. So maybe I should buy a farm in the stinking country and raise chickens. What happens when some guy from our old neighborhood is on the lam and needs a hideout? Do I turn him away from the door?

"Suppose I quit and go to Europe, maybe back to the old country, or to South America. Then I got narcotic agents on my tail half the time and every time I blow my nose it's a big deal. Like with Lucky. There ain't no out, Teresa. There ain't never been no out since I started. Sooner or later they'll frame me because I'll make good headlines and they can say the underworld is licked. Like they always say. And on the side they'll say to me like they said to Lucky, 'Sure this is a bum rap. But look at all the stuff you've been getting away with for years. You've got a stretch due you.' So I'll go to the can but the underworld will keep going. The ones who will take my place are growing up right now over in the slums where we was born. Over where another bunch of little snot-nosed bastards like I was are fighting in the gutter over a couple of pennies or snatching something to eat out of a store or getting their ears batted down by some potbellied flat-foot. Maybe like me they get so goddamned mad their guts ache and they promise themselves they won't always have to take it. They'll get even someday.

"They'll get even like I did!"

She didn't say anything. She just sat there, looking at me, her cheeks wet and shining in the light where she hadn't bothered to wipe away the tears. There was one more thing to say and then I was finished.

"You ain't never had no part of this. Not ever. You got your own life and your own way of helping people and it's a decent one. I shouldn't never have let you take a chance on ruining it. I went soft and made a mistake, but it ain't too late even now. We're through, do you understand? We're through!"

Her voice was like a choked whisper but I could hear it plain. Plainer than I had ever heard anything.

"No. No, Tony."

"Goddamn it, can't you understand English? Get out! Get out now and for good!"

When she just sat there without moving I turned while I still had the guts and headed for the little room off the entrance hall where Big Sam always sat in the evening in case the wrong parties should get too smart and try to see me alone.

"Go in there and throw that bitch out," I shouted at him. "Throw her out now."

He stared at me like I had gone nuts.

"You mean Teresa?"

"Can't nobody understand nothing in this goddamned place? For Christ's sake, get moving. Throw her out. Throw her out and don't never let her in again. You hear me? Don't never let her in again. Never!"

CHAPTER SIXTEEN

THREE WEEKS later the rumble started.

It began with a telephone call from Joe Santoro. He reached me at the cocktail lounge in the hotel where I spent an hour acting like a gentleman late every afternoon. He played it cagey from the start.

"I called up to break my date with you, Mr. Murray. Right now I don't feel so good and I think I'll sweat it out in a Turkish bath."

"That's O.K." I said. "Make it some other time."

I hung up slowly. Santoro didn't have no date with me. But it was easy figuring things out.

I waited ten minutes and then went out and walked down to the corner. At that hour all the taxis that went by had passengers and I stood in front of an apartment house until one pulled up to let out an old dame. Then I slid in and gave the address down on Second Avenue.

At the baths I got a room and undressed and wrapped a towel about me and went in to the pool. Santoro was already there, but so were two or three other characters. We passed a hello and let it go at that.

I took a dive into the pool and swam back and forth a couple of times and then got out and headed for the steam room. A minute later Santoro appeared.

"What gives, Joe?"

"I'm not certain yet, Tony. Something is in the wind and it don't smell good. Did you know you got a tail on you?"

"I figured maybe. That goddamned bunch of senators snooping around to make headlines. So what?"

"It ain't them. I mean, it ain't them alone. There's more than that to it, Tony."

"Stop talking riddles. You get me down here just to tell me some jerks want to put the finger on me?"

"It ain't that they just want to. They're doing it."

He gave it to me straight then, what he'd got from his contacts downtown. An assistant D.A. that was looking to make the right connections had spilled it to him.

"They got a special grand jury sitting, Tony, trying to pin a murder rap on you. You remember anybody named Vito Tramaglino?"

The goddamned steam was filling up my throat so I had to keep swallowing. I nodded and then remembered that Santoro couldn't see me clear. "I remember him."

"The Connecticut cops pulled a beer barrel with a body in it out of the Sound last year. Now they're saying it's what is left of this Tramaglino character."

"Who says so?"

"Cherry Nose Petrucci, for one. He says he walked with Tramaglino up to your office late one night and waited outside. But Tramaglino never walked out again. Instead you and Big Sam rolled a beer barrel out and loaded it on a truck."

I thought it over and came up with the only answer.

"Maybe Cherry Nose will have a different story before he ever gets up in court."

Only it seemed it wouldn't be that easy. Santoro gave me the rest of the setup. They had Cherry Nose in the can on a hi-jacking rap. Spilling his guts the way the D.A. told him was part of the deal to spring him.

"It's not just Cherry Nose alone talking," Santoro went on. "They got some flatfoot who swears he was a witness to you and Big Sam loading the barrel on the truck. It stayed in his mind because he'd never seen you do any heavy work before."

I started to say it had stayed in the bastard's head because he had got a bottle of good whisky out of it but then kept my mouth shut.

And then Santoro was saying, "On top of that, they've had the girl downtown a couple of times."

"What girl?"

"Tramaglino's sister. Teresa."

It was funny the way you could be sweating your goddamned blood out and at the same time feel cold inside like you had never felt before. My throat was tight all of a sudden as though the steam was choking me.

"What's that again?" Santoro asked.

"Nothing," I said. "I didn't say nothing."

That was what it was. Nothing. Mugs like Cherry Nose and the cop I could handle. They could be got to, no matter where they was hid out or how they was protected. But there was nothing I could do if Teresa had blown the whistle.

Santoro had other things to say but I was only listening with half an ear. They was just words he was using—words I could take hold of and understand later. But not right now.

Right now I just wanted to get alone somewhere. I didn't want having to watch my words and keeping hold of myself, the way I had kept hold of myself for years. Thinking twice before I did or said anything.

I got up slow from the wooden bench, waving the steam away from my face.

"Thanks, Joe. Dig up everything you can and keep in touch with me."

"I'll phone you like I did today at the hotel. The wires are tapped to your house phones."

"I figured."

I take the cold showers and the rubdown and dress and go home. So I'm alone again. Alone the way I'd always said guys like me ought to be. Sitting in the middle of a ten-room apartment that cost over a grand a month with maybe fifty, a hundred grand sunk in furniture and painted pictures. Legitimate stuff. Everything in the whole lousy dump legitimate.

I'm up on top. I can put my hands on two, three million in cash and more if I got a need to. I can give the nod and bury a thousand guys from here to the Coast and back again. There is Christ knows how many families in how many stinking slums that think I am God Almighty Himself. I'm Mr. Big, the one they all got to come to.

But there ain't nobody I can turn to. You get too far up and all of a sudden you are all by yourself.

I could hear Teresa's voice from a long time ago asking me, "What do they leave you, Tony? Did you ever ask yourself that? What do they leave you?"

So she had been someone to talk. She'd turned like they all turn. It wasn't no good blaming her—I was at fault. I'd known better, all along I'd known better.

Like I was always pounding into Big Sam.

"You can't trust nobody in this racket, Sam. Nobody. Keep that in mind and you won't never get double-crossed."

I didn't have no cause to bellyache now. I'd had the breaks for thirty years and it was time the dice started rolling the other way. And it didn't do no good asking over and over again why it had to be Teresa. She was human like anybody else.

That was what I kept telling myself the next two, three days while Santoro was slipping me information that was leaking to him out of the grand-jury room. The important thing was the date when Vito was killed and loaded into the barrel. The cop swore to it. Cherry Nose Petrucci swore to it. And they had Teresa back twice, questioning her.

"I don't figure it," Santoro told me. "They ought to have handed down an indictment by now, but something is holding it up."

"It don't matter. We'll take it as it rides."

And then one night late I hear a racket in the entrance hall to the apartment.

I'm just moving out to see what gives when Teresa comes running in. Big Sam is behind her, grunting and holding his belly.

"I tried to keep her out, Tony, but she give me the knee. I wasn't looking for no lady to do that."

He started after her then but I stopped him. "Forget it, Sam. I'll handle it from here on."

I waited until he was gone. I kept on waiting, not saying anything, leaving it to her to begin.

"I had to come, Tony. I had to talk to you. I tried to reach you on the telephone a hundred times but it didn't do any good."

"What makes you think this will do any good?"

She made an angry, impatient gesture with her hands the way old-country wops do.

"Stop acting tough! Tony, do you know what they're trying to do to you?"

"Somebody's always trying to do something."

"This is different. They had me downtown to the District Attorney's office. Talking about my brother. Saying you killed Vito."

I wet my lips with the tip of my tongue but then didn't say anything.

"They've got dates and witnesses, Tony," she went on in a rush. "What they call a circumstantial case. They thought they had everything."

It took a full minute for it to sink in. I turned it over in my mind and kept my voice careful.

"Thought?"

I hadn't moved from the chair in which I had been sitting when she came in, and she walked over and stood in front of me, staring down at me without any expression on her face.

"Listen to me carefully, Tony. They've had me downtown three times, trying to get me to change my story."

"What story?"

"The fact that Vito was alive for the next six months at least. He wrote me three or four times for money, and I saw him once when he came to New York for a day."

She said the words smoothly, evenly, as though she had said them so many times they came automatic. But to me they were words that didn't make sense. They were crazy.

I came half out of my chair, yelling at her. "What the hell are you trying to do? You never—"

It was the flat of her hand across my mouth that stopped me. Something that nobody had ever done since I was old enough to hit back.

"Goddamn you, shut up!" Her voice had a cold, deadly urgency. "Stop before you say anything, Tony! Stop and think. I've sworn to my testimony three times. You're the only one who can make a liar out of me. *The only one!*"

I sat there rubbing my hand over my face where she had hit me, staring at her quietly for a long time. Wiping thoughts I had had in my mind away and putting in fresh ones. You train yourself all your life not to trust no one and it is hard to begin. All your life you have been the one to do the protecting and work the angles and frame the alibis when they had to be framed.

And now Teresa was standing in front of me, wanting to fight me to make her lie stick, daring me to say different. Daring me to say for sure she was lying her heart out because the only way I could say it was to tell her flat I'd knocked Vito off myself.

I wet my lips again, but before I could say anything she cut in.

"Whatever it is, don't say it, Tony! Let me finish first. I've never asked you for anything important before, but this time I'm begging. Don't ever do anything or say anything, Tony, to make me have to change my story. Don't ever make me admit that I could have been wrong."

"Why?" I asked, when finally she stopped. "Why are you doing it?"

"Don't ask me that, either, Tony. Perhaps I understand some things better than you think—things that neither of us will ever be able to talk about. Perhaps I'm protecting a dream I once had—a dream I don't want ever to lose completely. A woman's reasons, Tony. Let it go at that."

All of a sudden I felt tired, more tired than I had ever felt in my life. Maybe it was because all at once I was realizing sharp and clear what it all meant. All my life I'd been fighting my way up, fighting and winning. Yet now I knew that from the start it had been in the cards that I should lose. You get too powerful and you have to lose. It couldn't be no other way.

"It won't do any good, Teresa," I said slowly. "No good at all. Sooner or later the pay-off always comes."

"But not this time, Tony! I won't let it."

This time or another didn't make no difference, I told her. You couldn't change the system. You couldn't change the way things worked.

"Sure I'll beat this rap, maybe. Even if it was true I could beat it, because you can always beat anything legitimate. But next time it won't be the same. It will be a frame, and a frame you can't never lick."

I turned away from her eyes and got up and went over to the phonograph. Sometimes when you had good music, real music, you could forget for a little while. Over my shoulder I said flatly. "They got to do something to me, baby. There's too many investigations going on. They're uncovering too much stinking rottenness and dirt. So they'll put me away and brush their goddamned hands off and say, 'See? We fixed everything.' That's what they've always done. That's what they'll always do. It ain't me personal that they want to wipe out, but their own dirt. With me gone they can pretend for a little while that they are clean. But they won't be. They won't never be!"

Behind me Teresa cried out something in a choked voice but I couldn't hear her plain. I had turned on the phonograph and was listening to Caruso going to work on *Pagliacci*.

Nobody never had a voice like him. Nobody.

THE END

www.ingramcontent.com/pod-product-compliance
Lightning Source LLC
Chambersburg PA
CBHW030124260626
47156CB00008B/2783